THE FAIRIES OF
SUNFLOWER GROVE

BOOK 1-6

PJ RYAN

PJRYANBOOKS.COM

BOOK 1: FIFI

ONE

"Faster, faster!" Fifi huffed and flapped her wings as hard as she could. The tiny fairy looked over her shoulder. Yes, Cara still flew only a short distance behind her. "Faster, faster!" She flapped her wings even harder and flew right into a spider web. "Ick! No! Ack!" She waved her hands through the web and fluttered her wings.

"Aw, too slow, Fifi!" Cara giggled as she zoomed past. "Watch out for that cranky spider!"

"Spider?" Fifi spun around in the web and saw more eyes than she could count staring back at her. "N-nice s-spider!" She shivered.

"You two again." The spider huffed and cut one of the sticky strands of web that held Fifi prisoner. "Always messing up my web! Go on! Get out of here!"

Fifi tried to fly, but her wings were still tangled in a sticky mess of web.

She tumbled far from the tall tree where the spider repaired his web. She fell down through leaves and bushes, until she slammed into the hard ground.

"Ouch!" She groaned. As she sat up, she rubbed her shoulder. Then she glanced around. The leaves above were much larger than her. She couldn't see past them. "Cara!"

She listened closely for the sound of flapping wings.

Instead, she heard a soft cry.

She pulled gooey handfuls of web off her wings as she walked toward the sound. She pushed back a large green leaf and saw a ladybug with a wilted pink petal in her hands. Big tears rolled down the ladybug's face.

"Oh dear, what's wrong?" Fifi rushed over to her.

"It's so sad, so very sad. I can't stop crying." The ladybug held out the petal. "Can you fix it?"

"I'm sorry." Fifi took the petal in her hands. She felt how dry and thin it was. "It's natural for flowers to lose their petals. But don't worry, more will bloom."

"Fairies have magic. You have to fix it!" The ladybug stomped her feet.

"Yes, I do have magic, but it's important for the petals to fall. They get the soil ready for the next spring." Fifi crouched down and ran her fingers through the soil. "See how soft it is? Next spring it will be ready for new flowers to grow."

"Listen, listen, listen! You're not listening!" The ladybug stomped her feet again. Then she fluttered past tall blades of grass and disappeared through a tangled bush.

"What a strange little bug." Fifi frowned. She looked at the petal in her hand. "It is a bit early for the petals to be falling." She let go and the petal drifted to the soil. She pulled the last bit of spider-web goo off of her wings, then she jumped up, ready to fly.

Just before her wings flapped, she heard another soft cry. Eager to help, she took too sharp a turn and lost her balance. She fell to the ground with a hard thump.

"Ouch." She sighed. "Just what is that ladybug up to?" She flew up into the air—past the tall blades of grass, past the tangled bush—toward the sound of the cry. As she looked down, she saw something that shocked her so much she forgot to flap her wings.

It wasn't until she hit the ground again that she blinked.

"Ouch," she mumbled as she got to her feet.

The soil wasn't soft at all. It was hard and dry. Wilted petals covered the ground as far as she could see. Flower stems bent in all directions, with no blooms on them. Not even a single blade of grass brightened the space.

In the middle of it all, the ladybug cried. She held another petal in her hand.

"You have to fix it!" She waved the petal in the air. "Fairies have magic, you have to fix it!"

"My, my." Fifi gulped. "How could this happen?" She ran her fingers through the soil. It cracked and crumbled like dust. In all of her ten years, she had never seen anything like it. "It's nowhere near time for the change of seasons, and even if it were, that is not what this is." She pinched one of the stems. It bent, then broke. "It's so strange, so awful."

"Yes, that's what I was trying to tell you!" The ladybug huffed. "Now, kindly fix it!"

"Of course I will." Fifi smiled.

As a fairy, she had a very special gift—the gift of magic. One of her most important jobs was to tend to the needs of soil, flowers, and plants.

She crouched down and sank her palms deep into the soil. She took a deep breath, then closed her eyes. Her wings began to flap, then another smaller set hidden underneath began to flutter. They fluttered faster than a hummingbird's. Her body began to glow as bright and warm as sunlight. The ground trembled beneath her fingertips. Fifi imagined flowers of every color, bright and beautiful, filling up the barren space.

Then she opened her eyes.

"Oh no!" She gasped as she saw the same wilted flowers, broken stems, and dry dusty soil. "How could this be?"

"You didn't fix it." The ladybug put her hands on her hips.

"I tried." Fifi's eyes widened. "Maybe I still have some of that icky gooey spider web on my wings. I'll try again."

She smiled at the ladybug as she wiped her wings clean. Then she sank her hands back into the soil. She took a deep breath and began to flutter her wings.

Just as she began to feel the warm glow, something struck her in the side and knocked her right off her feet.

"Ouch!" she groaned.

"What's happened here?" Cara offered her hand to Fifi. "I'm sorry I crashed into you. I was flying and looked down. I was so shocked, I forgot to flap!"

TWO

Fifi dusted off her dress. "I have no idea. I tried to fix it, but it didn't work."

"What do you mean it didn't work?" Cara laughed. "You must not have been paying attention. You probably did something wrong."

"I was paying attention, I promise!" Fifi frowned. "I did everything right."

"It's okay, Fifi, sometimes we all have trouble concentrating. Here, why don't we do it together?" Cara held out her hand.

"Yes, that has to work!" Fifi smiled as she took her friend's hand. Then she placed her other hand in the soil. She took a deep breath as Cara did the same.

A soft hum filled the air as their wings fluttered. They glowed as bright and warm as the sun.

The ground trembled and Fifi opened her eyes, eager to see something wonderful.

Instead, she saw the same drab and lifeless scene.

"This is impossible!" Cara gasped.

"The fairies have lost their magic!" The ladybug flew up

into the air. "The fairies have lost their magic!" she shouted as she flew higher.

"Stop! That's not true!" Fifi waved her hands in the air, but she couldn't bring herself to fly. Her heart was too heavy with sadness.

"Oh no, this is not good." Cara frowned. "We have to get back to the grove and tell Ava about this before she finds out from someone else. She's going to be so upset."

"But what if she asks us why we were out here all alone?" Fifi fluttered her wings. "We're going to get in trouble!"

"It doesn't matter." Cara shook her head. "We have to tell the truth. This is far more important than us getting into a little bit of trouble."

"You'll get into a little bit of trouble, I'll get into a lot!" Fifi sighed. "But you're right. We do have to tell her." She sniffled as she looked into Cara's eyes. "Do you think we've really lost our magic?"

"Let's find out." Cara pulled a seed out of her pocket. It filled up almost her whole palm. She covered it with her other hand and closed her eyes. Her wings fluttered so fast that she began to lift off the ground. Her hand glowed as warm and bright as the sun. "Did it work?" She squeezed her eyes shut as she landed back on the ground. "I'm too afraid to look." She slowly opened her hands.

"Yes!" Fifi smiled at the tiny sprout in Cara's hand. "It worked." She gave the tiny blossom a light tap with her fingertip. "Happy birthday, little one."

The little flower wrapped its stem around Fifi's finger, then wiggled its petals.

"See. All is well." Cara smiled as she slipped the sprout into her pocket.

"But it's not, Cara." Fifi frowned. "Yes, your magic worked on that seed. But what about this one?" She plucked a seed from the dusty soil. Then she closed her hand over it. She closed her eyes, fluttered her wings, then began to lift off the ground. She smiled as she felt warmth flow through her hands. When her feet touched the ground again, she kept her eyes closed. "Did it work?" She opened her hands.

"No!" Cara gasped.

"Oh no." Fifi looked at the unchanged seed in her hand.

"Are you sure you didn't lose some of your magic?" Cara placed her hands on her hips. "Did you get in trouble and not tell me?"

"No, I've been good, I promise!" Fifi slipped the seed into her pocket. "I think it's this place, Cara. Something is wrong here—very wrong! Magic doesn't work here."

"But that's not possible." Cara shook her head. "Magic works everywhere. The whole world is magic, Fifi."

"I know that, but it's not working here! What other explanation can there be?" Fifi shivered. "For some reason our magic can't fix this."

"Ava will know how to fix it. Remember, she is far wiser than us. We just have to get to her!" Cara zipped up into the air. "Let's go, Fifi!"

Fifi jumped into the air. Her wings fluttered, but she couldn't get very high before she fell right back down.

"I can't, Cara!"

"Fifi, there's no time for silly games!" Cara snapped her wings at her. "Let's go!"

Fifi tried to fly again. But each time she did, she felt too sad to flap her wings.

"I'm sorry, Cara, I just can't." She sniffled as tears filled her eyes.

"Oh, never mind!" Cara swooped down and grabbed Fifi by her arm. "I'll help you."

Fifi clung to her friend's arm as she zoomed off through the air. She looked back at the broken flowers as a tear rolled down her cheek.

Now she understood why the ladybug was so upset. It was terribly sad.

A few seconds later, the sky brightened, the ground below filled with bright and beautiful flowers. Cara zipped to the left toward the Grove.

Nestled between two large hills, a lake sparkled in the sunlight. Beyond the lake, a thick forest of trees stretched toward the sky.

Cara zoomed straight through a pile of leaves and through a secret door. Once inside, she let Fifi go.

The entire village glowed with the sunlight that streamed through thick leaves. Waterfalls tumbled down tall stones and filled a wide stream that ran the length of the grove. Huge flowers bounced and swayed in the light breeze above them.

"Isn't it good to be home?" Cara smiled. "Don't worry, Fifi, Ava is going to make everything better." She bolted off toward the palace.

Fifi followed after her, but she did worry. She worried about the ladybug and about the broken flowers. And she worried about her wings that wouldn't fly.

She knew that Ava, at one hundred years old, was the oldest fairy in the grove. Ava told tales of times that the young fairies could only imagine.

But never once, that Fifi could recall, had Ava told a tale like this.

THREE

Spiral seashells jutted up toward the sky from the top of the mushroom palace. The top of each mushroom came together to create a ceiling, with plenty of open air and open sky between them.

The closer she came to the palace, the more nervous Fifi felt.

She ran her hands along one of her wings and pulled it close so that it covered her face.

"It won't be that bad. It's a good thing that we found that place." Cara nudged her with her elbow. Then she followed a trail of tiny gold pebbles to the center of the palace.

"Ava?" Cara called out between long green blades of grass. "Are you here?"

"Who is that? Cara?" The blades of grass parted. Ava floated on a lily pad in the center of a puddle. Although the mushroom ceiling blocked out some of the sunlight, the water still sparkled.

"Yes, Ava, it's me—and Fifi." She nudged Fifi again. "Say hi!" she whispered.

"H-hi, Ava." Fifi hid behind her wing again.

She didn't often speak to Ava unless she was in trouble.

Though the wisest fairy was kind and fair, she expected all the fairies to follow the rules, especially the young ones.

Fifi liked rules. She liked to follow them. She just had a hard time remembering what they were.

"Fifi, why are you hiding?" Ava laughed. Then she looked at them both. "What's wrong? Has something happened?"

"We were out flying and we found something terrible." Cara frowned.

"Out flying? Where?" Ava flew up off of the lily pad, then landed right in front of them. "Are you hurt?"

"No, we're not hurt." Fifi sighed. "The truth is, I wanted to have a race."

"And we went a little too far." Cara squirmed.

"Past the hills?" Ava's eyes widened.

"Yes." Fifi frowned. "And I'm so sorry, but we have to tell you what we found. There are flowers—all wilted, their stems broken." She shivered as she remembered the sight of them. "The soil is like dust."

"Fifi!" Ava stared at her. "Are you making up this story because you know you flew further than you should?"

"She's not making it up. I saw it too." Cara fluttered her wings. "I've never seen anything like it before."

"Because it can't exist. Not here." Ava began to walk back and forth. "Are you sure it wasn't just a few blooms that fell early? The birds can be a little wild sometimes and knock off the petals."

"No, Ava." Fifi reached into her pocket and pulled out the seed she'd taken from the soil. "What's worse is that magic doesn't seem to work there."

"Nonsense!" Ava snapped her wings. "Magic works everywhere! That is like saying there is no air to breathe. Fifi, wild stories won't change the fact that you broke a rule."

"It's true! Look!" Fifi closed her hands over the seed. She took a deep breath. She fluttered her wings. She felt the glow. Then she opened her hands. "See? Nothing." She looked down at the seed in her hand.

"Nothing?" Ava peered at the seed. "Are you sure it isn't some rabbit poop?" She gave it a light poke.

"I'm sure!" Fifi scrunched up her nose at the thought. "It's a seed. I took it from the soil there. But it won't bloom."

"Where is this place?" Ava looked between them. "You must take me there at once!"

"I can show you!" Fifi started to fly up into the air. But seconds later she spiraled back down.

"That's the other thing." Cara flew up into the air. "Something is wrong with her wings."

"What did you get into, Fifi?" Ava hovered over her.

"A spider web." She frowned.

"I should have guessed. You stay here and take a bath. Cara will show me. But Fifi, listen close." She looked straight into the young fairy's eyes. "Not a word about this to anyone? Understand?"

"Yes, Ava." She nodded.

"I mean it. Until we find out what is really happening here, you must not tell anyone else." She reached down and touched Fifi's cheek. "Remember."

"I will, Ava, I promise." She watched as the two fairies flew off into the sky. Once more she tried to take off after them.

Though her wings flapped, she sank right back down to the ground. "Why won't you work?" She swatted at her wings. She didn't think the spider web had hurt them. She'd gotten stuck in many spider webs. Still, she walked off to the stream to take a bath. She hoped that by the time Ava returned with Cara, everything would be just fine again.

Surely, if anyone could fix it, Ava could. She knew how to

use her fairy magic in ways that made Fifi's head spin. She could only hope that one day she would learn to be as skilled. But at the moment, she couldn't even fly, let alone follow the rules. She doubted that she'd ever be the kind of important fairy that Ava had become.

She grabbed a bit of moss from the ground and slid into the cool water of the stream. She used the moss to scrub her wings. As she bathed, she thought about the tiny seed in her pocket and the broken flowers she'd left behind.

She knew she shouldn't worry, but she couldn't stop herself. What if Ava couldn't fix it either?

As sadness washed over her again, water splashed across her face.

"Hey! Watch it!" Fifi ducked as more water flew in her face.

FOUR

"So sorry, please forgive me!" a soft voice croaked. "I am on a hunt for the most delicious fly and it just happened to fly straight toward you!"

"Gupper?" Fifi wiped the water from her eyes and stared into the green face of a large frog.

"Hi, Fifi." He hopped onto the ground beside the river. "Drat, that pesky fly got away."

"You shouldn't chase them." Fifi shook her head. "They get so scared!"

"I can't help it, it's my nature." He flicked his tongue out, then tucked it back into his mouth. "My belly may always be full, but when I see those flies, I just have to hunt!"

"Silly Gupper, you'll never get one. They are protected by the fairies." She climbed out of the water and sat down beside him.

"I know. Such a good thing." He stretched his toes. "Why do you look so sad?"

"Because I saw a terrible thing today and—" She clamped her hands over her mouth.

"It's okay, you can tell me." He smiled.

"No, I really can't!" Fifi sighed. "Well, I'm not supposed to."

"Why don't we play a game?" Gupper bounced to his feet. "That always brightens you up. You be the fly and I'll be the frog!"

"Maybe." She fluttered her wings. "I need to test these out anyway." She launched into the air and began to flap her wings. She flapped as hard as she could, but she still fell right back to the ground. "It's no use. I can't fly at all."

"That's strange indeed. I've never heard of a fairy that couldn't fly. Maybe you need a bit of a kick?" He swung one of his feet through the air.

"No!" Fifi laughed as she jumped out of the way. "I don't think that will help. It was after I saw the wilted flowers—that's when I stopped being able to fly."

"The wilted flowers?" He crept closer to her.

"Oh no!" She gasped. "I wasn't supposed to say that."

"You've said it now, little fairy." He stared into her eyes. "You don't need to hide it from me, I've seen it too."

"You have?" She pointed in the direction of the wilted flowers. "Over there? Past the hills?"

"No. In another place. I'll show you." He turned and began to hop away.

"Wait! I'll never be able to keep up. I can't fly, remember?" She crossed her arms.

"Oh, right." He crouched down low. "Climb aboard, Fifi."

"Thank you, Gupper!" She climbed onto his back.

"Hold on tight! I don't need wings to fly!" He jumped through the air.

Fifi held on as Gupper jumped swiftly through the trees along the stream.

It wasn't long before they were in a part of the grove that she had never seen before. The trees grew tight together and there wasn't a lot of sunlight. Beetles crawled under leaves and snakes slithered into the stream.

"Gupper, is it okay to be here? Is this one of the forbidden places?"

"It's forbidden for you, but not for me. The creatures are hungrier here. It's not safe for tiny fairies. But with me, you'll be fine." He hopped a little further.

"Gupper, I'm already in trouble today; this is going to make it worse." Fifi frowned.

"I just want you to see this." He pulled aside some tall reeds and revealed what looked almost like a pond. Now it was no more than a few puddles and a lot of mud. "It's just gone." He looked up at her. "How does a pond just disappear?"

"I don't know." Fifi gazed at the muddy pit. "Take me back, Gupper. I need to tell Ava right away."

Gupper hopped back along the stream until he reached the mushroom palace.

"Fifi, there you are!" Cara swooped down to greet her, with Ava landing a few steps away.

"We've been looking for you." Ava frowned.

"Did you fix the flowers?" Fifi slid down off of Gupper's back. "There's another place that needs help too." She felt her face go warm as she looked over at the frog and then back at Ava. "I'm sorry, I might have forgotten not to tell anyone."

"It's alright, Fifi. It doesn't matter now. Everyone will know soon enough." Ava took a deep breath. "I couldn't fix them, and Cara and I saw many other patches of wilted flowers as we flew back here. I'm afraid that we have a big problem on our hands. But it's no concern of yours—or Cara's. The elder fairies and I will handle this. The two of you need to stay within the grove and go no farther than the hills. All the young fairies must follow this rule until this problem is fixed."

She snapped her wings, then flew off into the palace.

Fifi stared after her, too stunned to speak.

"It's bad, Fifi, very bad." Cara hugged her. "But I'm sure Ava and the elders will be able to fix it."

"I knew it," Gupper croaked. "After all these years. I can't believe she's back again."

"Who?" Fifi stared at him. "Do you know what's happening?"

"I don't know what's happening, but I'm sure I know who's behind it." Gupper nodded. "Bella."

"Bella? Who's that?" Fifi blinked.

"She was a young fairy like you. But she had some ideas that the other fairies didn't like. She wanted to use her magic in ways that aren't allowed. Ava took her magic away to keep the grove safe. Bella was so upset, she left the grove. No one has seen her since."

"Ava took all her magic?" Fifi's eyes widened. "I would be upset too."

"Ava did what was best." Gupper hopped off toward the stream. "Stay away from Bella, little fairy!"

FIVE

As the sun rose the next morning, the grove was already busy with fairies flying in all different directions. Ava and the other elders had gathered at the center of the grove within a ring of tall sunflowers.

"Fifi, did you hear?" Cara landed on the ground beside her.

"Hear what?" Fifi watched as the other fairies flew through the air.

"Ava is having a meeting. She says that all the fairies must come together to use their magic to protect the rest of the grove. Let's go, we can't be late!" Cara flew up into the air.

Fifi sighed. The first thing she'd done when she woke up that morning was try to fly. But she couldn't even get off the ground.

"I'll meet you there." She frowned. She didn't want the other fairies to know that she couldn't fly. She was already the forgetful fairy—the fairy who couldn't focus. She didn't want to be the fairy that couldn't fly too.

Cara waved to her as she flew off toward the sunflower circle.

Fifi started to follow after her, then she stopped. What if

Gupper was right? What if Bella was responsible? If Ava and the others used all their magic to try to protect the grove, Bella would just steal it and then the fairies would have no way to protect the grove or themselves.

But maybe Fifi could help in a different way.

If it was magic that Bella wanted, then she would keep stealing it from the grove. Since it was used to nurture nature, all of the flowers and plants were full of it.

"But what if we nurtured them in a different way?" She smiled at the thought.

It was a long walk but she returned to the wilted flowers. When she arrived, she looked at the dusty soil. "Plants can't grow without moisture."

She placed her hands on her hips and looked around. She saw an empty acorn shell. She picked it up and walked over to a nearby pond. She scooped up some water from the pond and filled the acorn shell.

When she returned to the dusty soil, she poured the water over it. The soil drank it up in a second.

"Oh dear, this is going to take a long time." She took a deep breath, then nodded. "But I can do it."

Fifi walked back to the pond, gathered more water, and poured it onto the soil.

As she continued to go back and forth, she began to have the feeling that someone was watching her.

When she returned to the soil with more water, a voice startled her.

"What are you doing, tiny fairy?"

The spider hung down from his web. He dangled right in front of Fifi's face.

"N-nice s-spider!" Fifi jumped back, her eyes wide.

"Don't be scared, little one." He drifted down to the ground.

"I've been watching you and I'm curious. Why are you bringing the water here?"

"The soil is dry. It needs water so that the plants can live." She looked into his many eyes. "My magic can't fix it, but my hands can." She held up the acorn shell.

"I see. Clever little fairy." He smiled. "I'll help you."

"Really? With all your legs you can probably carry a lot of water!" She grinned.

"I can. But I have another idea. Let me show you." He began to weave his web into a long tube that stretched from the pond to the dry soil. "There. Now pour your water in."

Fifi poured the water from the acorn shell into the tube. It splashed its way down to the dry soil. "How wonderful! Now I don't have to walk back and forth. What a great idea!"

"I thought you might like it." He smiled.

"What are you doing down there?" The ladybug swooped down from above them. "Are you saving the flowers?"

"We are trying!" Fifi waved to the ladybug, then scooped more water into the tube.

"I can help." The ladybug flew off.

"That's a strange way of helping." Fifi laughed. Then she scooped more water into the tube. A few seconds later the sky turned red. "What is that?" Fifi stared up at it.

Suddenly hundreds of ladybugs flew down from the sky. Three ladybugs carried one acorn shell and each trio scooped the water into the tube. Soon the tube was full of water, flowing down onto the dry soil.

"This is amazing!" Fifi clapped her hands. Then she noticed a puddle in the soil. "Oh dear, the water is only staying in one place. We need it to spread out."

"I can help," someone hissed.

Fifi jumped backwards and landed on her bottom. She

stared with wide eyes as a snake lifted her head and wiggled her tongue.

"I've been watching. We want our pond back and if you can fix this place, maybe you can fix our place too."

"I will try!" Fifi nodded and shivered.

"Don't be scared, little one." The snake slithered along the soil. "I can make grooves in the soil so the water can reach everywhere."

"Thank you!" Fifi watched as the snake slithered through the soil. The water began to flow in all directions.

"Fifi!" Cara's voice surprised her. "What are you doing out here? Ava has been looking for you!"

"Look, Cara, we're fixing it!" She smiled as she ran her fingers through the moist soft dirt. "See?"

"Oh, I see. I see very well." Ava flew up beside Cara and looked down at Fifi. "Young fairy, we need to talk."

SIX

Fifi's wings fluttered nervously as she followed Ava away from the others.

"Ava, I'm sorry. I know you said to stay, but I just wanted to try to do something good!"

"You did something good. Very good." Ava smiled. "The soil will be rich and perhaps it will be well. But there is a bigger problem we all face."

"Bella?" Fifi pulled one of her wings around her. "Is she the problem?"

"How do you know about Bella?" Ava stared at her, then shook her head. "Never mind, it's best that you do know. If you happen to see her, you must stay far away from her. She's stealing magic wherever she can get her hands on it."

"But isn't she a fairy just like us?" Fifi let her wing unfurl.

"She is a fairy, yes, but she didn't want to follow the rules." Ava sighed. "We have rules for a reason, you know."

"Yes." Fifi frowned. "I know I broke another rule today."

"What made you think of this idea?" Ava peered at Cara as she tossed an acorn shell full of water down the spider-web tube.

"I just thought that the less magic we use, the less magic Bella would be able to steal."

"That is a brilliant idea, Fifi. Let's go back now."

Ava guided Fifi back toward the group of ladybugs, the spider, and the snake. She spread her hands to all who had gathered. "Thank you all for your help. I hope that you will continue to work with us as we get through this difficult time."

"Anything we can do to help, Ava," the spider said and bowed.

"Together we can fix it!" the ladybugs chirped.

"Happy to s-share my s-services," the snake hissed.

"There's something I want to try." Fifi pulled the seed from her pocket. She planted it in the damp soil, then she stood back and smiled. As she stared at the soil, her smile faded. "Nothing's happening."

"It takes time, sweetheart." Ava put her arm around Fifi's shoulder. "Our magic helps things grow faster, but without it, it will take time for the seed to sprout."

"But will it grow?" Fifi looked into her eyes.

"Maybe in time it will grow. We'll just have to wait and see. In the meantime, we will all keep taking care of our plants this way." Ava took a deep breath, then snapped her wings. "We have a lot of work to do!"

"On it!" Fifi laughed and ran toward the spider-web tube. She grabbed an acorn shell and filled it with water.

For a moment she forgot that she couldn't fly, and she launched into the air. Her wings fluttered a few times. She glided a short distance, then she dropped down fast and landed right on the edge of the tube.

"Oh dear, oh no!" Fifi lost her balance and toppled forward. She slid right down the tube and splashed into the soil.

"Fifi, are you okay?" Cara gasped.

"I'm great! That was so much fun! You have to try it!" She laughed as she stood up dripping wet.

"Really?" Cara squinted at her. "Are you sure?"

"I promise!"

"Fifi." Ava caught her hand. "You still can't fly?"

"No, Ava." Fifi frowned. "I scrubbed my wings, just like you said I should, but I still can't fly."

"Oh." Ava tugged at one of her wings. "Do they hurt?"

"No. They flap just fine. See?" She flapped her wings so fast that droplets of water went flying everywhere around her.

"Okay, I see!" Ava jumped out of the way of the water.

"Do you know why I can't fly, Ava?" Fifi folded her wings. "Is it because I broke too many rules?"

"No, that's not it at all." Ava touched her cheek. "I'm not sure why you can't fly. But we'll figure it out. I promise. Remember what I said, Fifi. Stay away from Bella."

Ava zipped up into the air, then flew off.

Fifi turned around in time to see Cara splash out of the end of the tube.

"That was fun!" Cara laughed as she jumped to her feet. "It's your turn!"

"No, that's okay." Fifi hung her head. "I don't want to do it anymore. It's getting too dark for everyone to work. I'm just going to go home and go to bed."

"Don't be sad." Cara hugged her. "You're going to fly again soon. I just know it. Look what you did today!" She pointed to the moist soil. "You did this—not with magic, just with your own hands."

"Not without help." Fifi smiled.

"Yes, everyone helped, but it was your idea. Without it, the soil would still be dusty and dry and there would be no chance of the seed growing." Cara tugged her hand. "Let's go, I'll fly you home."

"No thanks. Thank you for trying to cheer me up, but I'm just going to walk."

Fifi walked away from Cara, her heart still heavy. She hoped the seed would grow. She was glad that so many creatures had worked together to fix the soil. But she still had a big problem.

If her wings worked, why couldn't she fly?

She thought about this as she wandered toward the grove—at least she thought she was heading toward the grove. At some point she must have gone left instead of right.

Everything became very dark. When she looked up, she couldn't see the moon past the leaves.

Her heart pounded. Was she in the forbidden place?

"My, my, little fairy, you must be lost."

A sinister giggle filled the air.

SEVEN

"Who said that?" Fifi spun around in a circle. "Who's there?" She peered up through the thick leaves and branches.

"Don't you know not to wander here?" Glowing eyes stared down at her from a branch above her head.

"I got lost." Fifi sighed. "I have a hard time paying attention and remembering things."

"Why not just fly away?" The eyes peered at her.

"I can't fly." She ran her hands along one of her wings.

"Nonsense." The eyes blinked, then swooshed down toward her.

Fifi gulped and jumped back. "Who are you?"

"If you're so scared, then fly!" The creature stayed in the shadows.

"I can't!" Fifi stomped one foot. "I already said that!"

"But it's impossible. You're a fairy."

Fifi felt a light tug on one of her wings. "Hey!" She spun around to find the glowing eyes again. "You're the one that won't show yourself. Are *you* scared?"

"Me? Scared?" Another giggle filled the air. "No, I'm not afraid of anything." She stepped out of the shadows.

"You're a fairy?" Fifi's eyes widened as she saw the other fairy's long wings.

"Why yes, I am." She fluttered her wings. "At least I'm supposed to be." She crossed her arms.

"But I know all the fairies! I've never seen you in the grove." She frowned, then her heart pounded. "Bella? Are you Bella?"

"Ah, so you've heard of me?" Bella smiled. "I guess you know how terrible and horrible I am."

"I have to get back." Fifi stumbled as she took two steps back. She wanted to run, but she didn't want to be rude.

"In such a hurry now?" Bella followed after her. "Why not stay and make a new friend? Or did the elder fairies tell you to stay away from me?"

"It's late, I need to go home." Fifi turned to run. She felt a hand on her shoulder before she could.

"I was a fairy just like you once." Bella stepped up beside her. "I had magic." She spread her hands out before her. "But the elder fairies didn't like me. In fact, none of the other fairies liked me either. They took away my magic." She balled her hands into fists. "Do you know what that feels like?"

"N-no." Fifi shivered as she tried to imagine it.

"I haven't felt warm since." Bella rubbed her hands along her arms. "It's like all of the sunshine is gone."

"Is that why you've been stealing it?" Fifi glared at her. "You're the reason for the broken flowers and the dried-up pond!"

"I had no choice." Bella snapped her wings. "A fairy can't survive without magic."

"It wasn't yours to take!" Fifi crossed her arms.

"Well, I don't have to worry about that anymore." Bella smiled.

"What do you mean?" Fifi stared at her.

26

"I have all the magic I need now." She snapped her fingers and a large net made of spider web dropped down over Fifi.

"No! Let me out!" Fifi gasped as she tried to get free of the web. The more she fought against the sticky stuff, the more stuck she became. "Bella, you can't do this!"

"Why not?" Bella giggled. "You're not exactly a good fairy, are you, Fifi? You can't even fly."

"You know my name?" Fifi froze.

"I know every fairy's name. I've been watching all this time. It took me many years, but I finally figured out how to draw the magic that's left behind from the flowers and the plants. Now I have magic again. Lucky for me, I know how to draw it out of fairies too." She smiled. "Get comfortable in there, Fifi, it's your new home."

Fifi's heart ached. How could this be her new home? Tears rolled down her cheeks. She wished she had flown back to the grove with Cara. She wished she'd run away when she first realized it was Bella who'd spoken to her. She wished that her wings would work, so that she could fly far away from the meanest fairy she'd ever met.

Instead, she was trapped.

She wiped her tears away and took a deep breath. Even if she couldn't fly, she still had magic.

She held up her hands toward the spider web and closed her eyes. Soon her hands began to glow. She imagined the spider web breaking apart.

When she opened her eyes again, she found that the web was still there.

"No, that's not going to work, sorry." Bella flitted past her. "That's not just any spider web. It's a magic spider web. Magic can't work against magic."

"Bella, please, you have to let me go!" Fifi sniffled. "This isn't the way to get your magic back."

"As if there is any other way?" Bella laughed. "Sit tight, little fairy, you'll be put to work soon enough."

Bella flew off into the darkness.

Fifi sat down and hugged her knees. She did her best not to cry. She thought about screaming, but she was too far away for anyone to hear her.

She was all alone. Bella would never let her go.

"You can't give up, Fifi," she whispered. "It may look bad right now, but things always get better."

An owl screeched loudly in the distance.

Fifi jumped and covered her head. She sniffled again. Things sure didn't seem to be getting better.

She thought about what Bella had said. None of the fairies liked her. Bella must have felt just as alone as Fifi did. She must have wondered if things would ever get better. She said she wasn't scared of anything, but when she was a young fairy, had she been afraid?

Fifi certainly was afraid. She closed her eyes tight and wished that Cara was there beside her. Cara always helped her, no matter what trouble she got into. But there was no way her friend could find her now.

"Little fairy, what are you doing out here?"

The soft voice drifted to her from behind some tall reeds.

EIGHT

"Gupper!" Fifi jumped to her feet. "Gupper, is that you?"

"Yes, it's me."

Fifi watched as the frog pushed his way through the reeds.

"It looks like you've gotten yourself in quite a bind."

"Please, help me get out!" Fifi waved her hands in the air. "I can't use magic to free myself."

"I warned you, didn't I?" He hopped around the spider-web cage. "I said, stay away from Bella."

"I tried to!" Fifi sighed. "I did!"

"You shouldn't have been wandering, little fairy." He flicked his tongue, then smiled. "Now you see why this is the forbidden place."

"I see. Yes. Gupper, please get me out!" Fifi flapped her wings as he continued to hop.

"I'm afraid I can't do that." Gupper stopped in front of the cage. "You belong to Bella now."

"Gupper. You're my friend!" Fifi gasped.

"I am your friend. I told you to stay away. But Bella is in charge of the forbidden place. I have to do what she says. She has magic and she's not afraid to use it." He frowned. "I'm sorry, Fifi, but I can't help you."

"B-but you have to! How else will I get free? My magic doesn't work!" Fifi pushed her hands against the sticky spider web. "Please!"

"Magic isn't the only way, little fairy. I heard about the way you softened the soil and the seed you planted. You didn't do that with magic, did you?" He smiled. "I can't help you, Fifi; I wish I could. But I know you'll find your way out."

"How?" Fifi ripped her hands free of the sticky mess. "She's going to come back, Gupper. She's not going to let me go!"

"I know." He sighed. "She's been hoping to catch a fairy. You are her prize. I'll do what I can, little fairy, but you're going to have to find a way to save yourself." He hopped off through the reeds again.

Fifi's heart sank. The moment she'd seen Gupper she thought she was saved, but now she knew that help likely wouldn't come.

She sat down and began to cry. As she pulled her wings around her, she wished that she were anything but a fairy. She wished she were a beetle that could crawl away or a bird with a strong beak to break through the web.

Instead, she had sticky hands and broken wings.

"He's right." She whispered. "I never should have wandered. I should have stayed in the grove where I was safe."

"The grove isn't so great," Bella called out as she landed beside Fifi's webbed cage. "All those rules—they can really get you down."

"I don't mind." Fifi jumped to her feet. "Please, Bella, let me go. I'm not the fairy you want. I'm not a good fairy at all. I can't even fly! I always forget things. I'm always doing something wrong. I don't even know how to use my magic to do most things!"

"Is that what they tell you?" Bella peered through the tangled spider web at her. "That you're not a good fairy?"

"Well, no." She frowned. "No one says it. They don't have to. I can tell."

"They said it to me. I wanted to use magic to create mystical creatures. I wanted to change the color of the water and turn the raindrops into snow. I just wanted to have a little fun." Bella huffed. "But no, the elder fairies told me it wasn't allowed. When I tried anyway, that's when they took my magic. I was just curious!"

"I've never thought about making mystical creatures or changing the color of the water." Fifi's eyes widened. "What a wonderful imagination you must have."

"What?" Bella glared at her. "Why would you say that?"

"Because it's true. To dream of turning raindrops into snow? Why, you must be very special. Did you have any other ideas?" She crept closer to the edge of the cage.

"Yes, lots. I wanted to paint the flowers with polka dots. I wanted to teach every fairy how to hop and slither like the frogs and the snakes. I wanted to teach them how to sing and chirp like the birds and the crickets. But the elder fairies said my ideas were silly. They said that hopping and slithering were for frogs and snakes and singing and chirping were for birds and crickets. They told me to learn my magic instead. But it was so boring." She groaned. "I didn't want to spend my day making seeds grow that would grow just fine on their own without me."

"That's true." Fifi smiled, even though she was frightened. "I just planted one today." Her smile faded as she remembered why. "But all of your ideas were wonderful. Why are you destroying everything now? Why would you want to hurt the creatures you love?"

"Why shouldn't I?" Bella snapped her wings so loudly that the ground shook.

"Bella!" Fifi gulped as she fell to her knees. "How did you get so powerful?"

"There's a little thing the elder fairies don't tell you, Fifi. Magic can be used any way you please. It doesn't have to nurture, it doesn't have to create rainbows or grow sprouts. It's your choice how you use it." She smiled as she clasped her hands together. "I chose to use mine to take back what was stolen from me. They told me I would never be a good fairy. The other fairies teased me all the time because I didn't want to dance or race. They said I wasn't like them. And they were right." She fluttered her wings until she hovered above the cage. "And it's time I showed them just how bad a fairy I can be!"

"Bella, please don't!" Fifi looked up at her. "Don't hurt anyone. It wasn't right for them to treat you like that. They were wrong. You are a good fairy!"

"If I'm such a good fairy, then why are you so scared?" Bella giggled. Then she touched the top of the spider-web cage with her hands.

As she did, the cage began to glow. Fifi began to glow too. As the warmth flowed through her, she felt it leave through the top of her head and the tips of her fingers.

NINE

Fifi knew that Bella was draining her magic. She could feel it. She was so dizzy, she couldn't speak. Just when she thought she would fall asleep, the magic stopped flowing.

She looked up at Bella and saw her hands stop glowing. She saw a spark in her eyes. Was that fear?

"Bella." Fifi pushed herself to her feet. "I'm sorry you're so afraid. No one should be that afraid."

"Afraid?" Bella giggled. "I told you, I'm not afraid of anything!"

"But you are." Fifi shivered as she felt just how afraid Bella was. "I can feel it. I've never felt anyone so afraid before. It must be very difficult to be all alone. Don't you have any friends at all?"

"I don't need friends." Bella crossed her arms. "Everyone here does what I say."

"Because they're scared. When I'm scared, my friend Cara always helps me feel better." Fifi looked into Bella's eyes. "Hasn't anyone ever helped you to feel better?"

"I don't need any help!" Bella huffed. "I am just fine on my own!"

"No, you're not." Fifi sniffled. "I'm sorry. I know how hard it can be to be different. None of the other fairies are forgetful like me. They can remember all the rules and they never get lost. Sometimes I feel like I'll never be a good fairy. It makes me so sad." She ran her hands along her wings. "And now I can't even fly."

"Is that true?" Bella sank down to her feet and stared through the cage at her. "I've never met another sad fairy before."

"It's true. But I'm never sad for long. Cara always cheers me up. I don't know what I would do without her." She frowned.

"Nobody would ever want to be my friend." Bella sighed. "But that doesn't matter. All that matters is that I'm in charge now. When I'm done with that grove, it'll be my home again and the rest of those fairies will be the ones that have to find a new place to call home." She jumped up into the air, ready to take flight.

"Wait, Bella!" Fifi pushed her hand through the sticky web. It was icky, it was gooey, and it was all over her fingers, but she still pushed until she finally got her hand to the other side. "Bella, I want to be your friend."

"Liar!" Bella shook her head. "Why would you want to be friends with a fairy like me? A fairy who locked you up? A fairy that wants to destroy everything? You're just trying to trick me!"

"No, I'm not." Fifi stretched her hand out to her. "I want to be friends with a fairy who has a wild imagination and great ideas. I want to be friends with a fairy who isn't scared of anything, even the forbidden place. I want to be friends with a fairy who wants to sing like the birds and slither like the snakes. I can't think of anyone more interesting!"

"That's silly." Bella sank back down to the ground again. She stared at Fifi's gooey hand. "No wonder you're always getting into trouble. You're not very smart, are you? Why would you want to be friends with a bad fairy like me?"

"Because you're not a bad fairy at all." Fifi smiled. "You're just different—like me. If you let me out, I can help you."

"You would help me?" Bella gasped. "Even though you know my plans?"

"I want to help you." Fifi nodded. "Please? We can be friends. And together, we can fix everything."

"You would use your magic to help me?" Bella waved her hand and the spider-web cage began to dissolve.

"Yes, Bella. I'll use anything I can to help you." Fifi smiled as the rest of the cage disappeared. "Let me be your friend."

"Let's go. We have a lot of work to do." Bella grabbed Fifi's hand. Then she launched into the sky.

As her wings flapped, they soared higher and higher.

"Fifi!" A tiny voice cried out from the ground.

Fifi looked down and saw Cara, her eyes wide as she stared up at them. Ava stood a few steps behind her.

Fifi realized they must have come to save her. Gupper had been brave enough to tell the truth, even though he was scared of Bella.

But they had arrived too late.

Fifi held tightly to Bella's arms as she flew. She started to call out to Cara, but closed her mouth tight. If Bella discovered the other fairies were there, she would try to hurt them. Fifi couldn't let that happen.

Fifi saw Ava wrap an arm around Cara's shoulder as they both looked up at Bella and Fifi. Then she watched them fly off together.

She couldn't forget the look in Cara's eyes. Had she heard Fifi promise to be Bella's friend? Had Ava?

Fifi's heart raced. She knew that if she was ever going to do anything right in her life, it had to be this. She hoped that she could.

Bella landed not far from the mushroom palace. She dusted off her wings and smiled. "With you at my side, we're going to change everything."

"Yes, I'm sure we will." Fifi took a deep breath. "Are you happy to be back home?"

"I am." Bella glanced around. "It's been so long. But everything looks the same."

"What's the plan, Bella?" Fifi began to pace back and forth. "Are you just going to scare everyone away?"

"No." Bella crossed her arms. "I'm going to destroy it all. Starting with the mushroom palace!"

Fifi gulped as Bella raised her hands into the air and began to direct her magic toward the tallest of the mushrooms.

"Bella, wait!"

TEN

Fifi jumped in front of Bella. The stream of magic that flowed from Bella's hands struck Fifi hard. She gasped as a terrible feeling rushed through her. Her eyes filled with tears.

"Bella, is this how you feel all the time?"

"What are you doing?" Bella growled. "Get out of my way!"

"I can't!" Fifi looked into her eyes. "I promised to be your friend and I'm going to be!"

"My friend wouldn't stand in my way!" Bella snapped her wings.

"Yes she would, if she knew what you were doing wasn't what you wanted!" Fifi crossed her arms and stared hard at Bella. "I know that you were hurt, but this isn't the way to fix it. If you let me, I will help you make it better."

"What can you do to make it better?" Bella snarled. "You tricked me! I knew it! You're just like the rest of them!"

"Bella!" Ava and the other elder fairies gathered at the top of the tallest mushroom. "You must stop this now!"

"Never!" Bella zipped up into the air. "You can't tell me what to do anymore!"

"Bella!" Fifi tried to fly up to her, but she could only hover. "You are my friend! I want to help you, but this isn't the way!"

"It's the only way!" Bella yelled.

"When we have a problem, we all work together to fix it. You can't do this alone. If you let us help you, we can fix it." Fifi stretched her hands up to her and felt them begin to glow. "You don't have to be alone anymore, Bella."

"You're lying! That's enough!" Bella shot a stream of glowing golden magic straight toward Fifi.

Fifi dove out of the way and landed in a pile of flowers.

"Ouch!" She huffed, then pushed herself to her feet. She plucked one of the flowers, then placed her hand on its petal. As her hand began to glow, she closed her eyes and hoped that it would work. When she opened her eyes again, she smiled. "Bella, look!" She thrust the flower into the air and waved it. "This is for you! A gift, because I am your friend!"

"A gift?" Bella swooped down closer. "Is this another trick?"

"No, Bella. Look." She held out the flower to her. Each of its long orange petals had blue polka dots scattered across it. "Isn't it beautiful?"

"Yes...yes, it is." Bella sniffled as she took the flower. "It's just like I imagined."

"I do understand you." Fifi wrapped her arms around Bella in a tight hug. "I don't want you to be alone anymore. I don't want you to be sad. I want you to know that you have a friend."

"A friend?" Bella whispered.

"We need a fairy just like you. A fairy that sees things in a different way. A fairy full of wonderful ideas. A fairy brave enough to try new things." Fifi hugged her even tighter and felt warmth flow through her.

As she began to glow, she could sense that Bella glowed too. Her heart filled with joy as her new friend hugged her back.

"Fifi! Get down here this instant!" Ava shouted.

"Get down here?" Fifi opened her eyes. She gasped as she saw the ground far below her. "Bella, why did you fly so high?" She clung to her friend.

"I didn't." Bella fluttered her wings. "I'm not flying at all, Fifi. You are!"

"I am?" Fifi's eyes widened as she flapped her wings. She gulped as she heard Ava shout again. "We have to go back. But don't worry. No matter what happens, I'll be by your side. Okay?"

"Okay." Bella took a deep breath.

They sank down to the tallest mushroom and settled right in front of Ava and the other fairies.

"Ava, I can explain!" Fifi held up her hands and began to speak. "Bella has some different ideas, but they're really great ideas and I think if we just give her a chance to share them, all this can be fixed. She's not a bad fairy at all, I promise. She just needs friends!"

"Silence!" Ava placed one hand on Fifi's shoulder, then looked into her eyes. "There are no bad fairies, dear. Not a single one."

"That's not true!" Bella crossed her arms.

"It is true." Ava offered her hand to Bella. "None of us ever wanted you to go away. When your magic was taken away, it was only to give you time to learn how to use it properly. Magic must be used with your heart, not because you want to show off. If you use it with your heart, it can cause no harm. But if you use it in other ways, it can hurt you and it can hurt others. I'm afraid you stopped using magic with your heart because the other fairies didn't treat you very nicely. We all have many things to learn and being kind to one another is one of the most important things." Ava smiled as she took Bella's hand. "I think you've learned that now, thanks to a wonderful fairy with a very special gift."

"Who?" Fifi blinked. "Cara? It was Cara, wasn't it? I knew she'd fix everything!" She smiled and waved to her friend.

"No, Fifi. Cara has her own very special gift. But it was you that had just the right one to save our grove and to save Bella." Ava took Fifi's hand. "Magic is a gift, but each fairy has one special talent of her own. Magic couldn't fix this, but your heart could, Fifi. I know that you sometimes forget things and it's hard for you to focus, but do you know why that is?"

"No." Fifi frowned.

"It's because you have a very big heart." Ava squeezed her hand. "You have a heart that feels more than other fairies do. It can be distracting. But because of your big heart, you felt how alone Bella was. That's why you couldn't fly. Your heart was too heavy. You were sad for the plants, yes. But you were also sad for Bella. Thanks to you, Bella learned something very important. Didn't you, Bella?" Ava looked over at her.

"Yes." Bella smiled. "I learned that the most powerful magic is friendship. I'm sorry for all the damage I caused." She sighed. "If you can't forgive me, I understand."

"I can." Ava hugged her. "We all can."

All of the fairies gathered close.

"Really?" Bella's smile grew wider.

"We promise to be your friends, Bella." Cara hugged her. "Together we can fix this."

"And then we can talk about your new ideas." Ava looked at the polka-dot flower. "I think it's time some things changed around here."

Fifi fluttered her wings and flew up into the air. She looked down at the fairies and smiled.

Maybe she was a little different. But maybe everyone else was a little different too—just like her. She felt a new sense of wonder as she thought about what each fairy's special gift might be.

BOOK 2: BELLA

CHAPTER 1

Big bulging eyes stared up at Bella from the sand beneath her feet. Not far away, a clear blue stream splashed along shiny rocks of all different colors as it ran through Sunflower Grove.

Bella barely noticed the splashing or the shiny rocks. Her attention was locked to the picture that unfolded in the sand. Long teeth hung from between two thin lips.

"Oops, I forgot the ears!" She laughed, then used the stick she held to draw two large cat-like ears on top of the oval head. "Just right." Bella tossed the stick down and smiled as she looked at her creation.

Fifi flew down from the bright blue sky and landed just behind Bella. "That is the strangest thing I've ever seen!" She folded her wings as she peered over Bella's shoulder. "Is it from a nightmare?"

"A nightmare?" Bella squeaked as her eyes widened. "No! Of course not. He's my friend." She scrawled the name JoJo across the sand above the creature's head.

"You've met this beast?" Fifi sat down in the sand beside her and continued to stare at the picture. "Where?"

"Not yet, I haven't." Bella used her fingertip to add more

spikes to the creature's fur. "But soon, I hope. I just started drawing him today. I can't wait to meet him."

"Bella, how are you going to meet him?" Fifi gave her a strange look.

"I can use my magic to make him come alive. Want to see?" Bella grinned as she started to wave her hand over the drawing.

"No, don't!" Fifi caught her hand and held it tight. "Bella, you can't just do that. It's not safe."

"There's nothing to be scared of—nothing at all." Bella pulled her hand away and shot Fifi an annoyed frown. "He's a sweet little thing, he can't hurt anyone."

"Those teeth don't look very sweet to me." Fifi scrunched up her nose.

"I'm sure we fairies look pretty strange and scary to other creatures. But we're nothing to be afraid of, are we?" Bella huffed, then snapped her wings sharply. "I should have known you wouldn't understand."

"I do think it's a great drawing." Fifi frowned. "I just don't think you should bring him to life. At least not until you ask Ava."

"I'm not going to ask Ava." Bella put a finger to her lips as the other fairies began to fill the sandy beach beside the stream. It was time for morning gathering and Ava would soon arrive to share some words of wisdom with them. "Not a word. It has to be a secret. Promise?" She held up her pinky finger.

"I promise." Fifi sighed and hooked her pinky finger around Bella's. She brightened up at the sight of her friend Cara fluttering toward them. "Cara! Over here!"

"Not even to Cara." Bella nudged Fifi's side with her elbow.

"Ouch! Watch it!" Fifi huffed, then fluttered away from Bella, but not far enough away that Bella couldn't still hear the two whisper.

"Are you okay?" Cara frowned as she looked past Fifi at Bella. "Did she hurt you?"

"No, she didn't. It's okay. We were just playing." Fifi smoothed down her wings.

Bella bit into her bottom lip as she watched them. Fifi and Cara were very good friends. They spent a lot of time together. Ever since Bella returned to Sunflower Grove, Fifi had been a good friend to Bella. But whenever Cara came around, the two would pair up like peas in a pod.

Bella knew that the other fairies still weren't too sure about her. They'd been nothing but nice to her ever since she was welcomed back, but she doubted that they all trusted her.

Fifi was the only fairy that really seemed to like Bella. But did she like her enough not to tell on her about JoJo?

Ava, an elder fairy and the leader of the grove, swooped down from the sky and landed in front of the gathering of fairies.

"Good morning, everyone!" She fluttered her wings so fast that they hummed.

The sound drew the attention of the fluttering, chattering fairies. Soon everyone was quiet.

"I have something very important to talk to you about today." Her honey-sweet voice drifted over the group. "As fairies, we all have access to something very special. Does anyone know what that is?"

"I do, I do!" Missy waved her hand in the air. She was the tiniest of all of the tiny fairies and also the youngest. She liked to be the first to answer questions and the first to offer to help. "Me, me!" She waved her hand fast.

Bella did her best not to roll her eyes. The question was boring and simple. Of course she knew the answer. It was always the same one. Sometimes she wished that Ava would be just a little more creative.

"Okay, Missy. What's the answer?" Ava smiled at her.

"Magic!" Missy shot sparkly rainbows out of her palms straight into the air as she spoke.

"That's right, Missy." Ava laughed and jumped out of the way of the rainbows. They arched across the stream, then burst into golden dust that scattered through the air.

Many of the fairies clapped and squealed with glee over the sight.

But not Bella. She sighed. Another sparkly rainbow. She was pretty sure that as long as there were fairies there would never be a shortage of sparkly rainbows. She didn't have anything against sparkly rainbows, but they were just so boring. Anyone could make a sparkly rainbow. What about all the things that hadn't been made yet?

"Magic is fun. I will admit that." Ava clasped her hands together as she hovered a few inches above the ground. "But it's far more than that. It's every fairy's job to know how to use this magic. It's not a toy. It's a responsibility. That's why young fairies start out with just enough, and as they learn and grow, they get more and more. What do you think would happen if a young fairy suddenly had all the magic of an elder fairy?" Ava drifted through the gathering of fairies. "Does anyone have any ideas about that?" She paused right in front of Bella.

CHAPTER 2

Bella hummed to herself as she imagined what it would be like to play with JoJo. She pictured his bright orange, spiky fur. She dreamed of staring into his deep green eyes. His furry clawed hands could dig giant holes in the sand, she was sure of it.

"Bella, are you listening?" Ava snapped her wings as she hovered before her.

Bella jumped suddenly and nearly fell backwards in her attempt to create some distance between herself and the elder fairy. But she only succeeded in bumping into the fairy behind her.

"Sorry, Ava." She frowned. "I am listening."

"Good, because this is very important..." Ava stared into her eyes. "...for every fairy to know." She tipped her head to the side. "What do you think would happen if a young fairy had all the magical power of an elder fairy, without any of the wisdom of how to use it?"

Bella's mind filled with ideas. With that much magic, a fairy could create just about anything, even an entirely new world. The thought made her imagination run wild. But she guessed that Ava was hoping for a different answer.

"I guess that the young fairy would probably create things she shouldn't." Bella shrugged.

"Very possible." Ava nodded slowly. "Although our magic can create many things, it's important to think about the consequences of everything we create. Nothing comes without a price."

"Ava?" Bella raised her hand high in the air.

"Yes, Bella?"

"How do we know what the price will be?" She stared at the fairy who was many decades older than her.

"That is the hardest part. As long as we create things out of love, in most cases, the price will be fair and balanced. But if it isn't love that goes into our creation, then the price can be quite high." Ava waved one finger through the air as she smiled. "Always ask yourself—is this creation good for me? Is it good for all the fairies? Is it good for the grove? Is it good for our whole world? If you can answer yes to all these questions, then you will be in pretty good shape."

"So, we can't create anything?" Bella blurted out with a sigh.

"What do you mean?" Ava fluttered over to her.

"It just seems impossible! How can anything be that perfect? How can I know for sure that all of the answers will be yes?" She shook her head. "You might as well just say we're not allowed to create anything that doesn't already exist. Or maybe nothing other than sparkly rainbows." She rolled her eyes.

"Oh, you can create much more than sparkly rainbows." Ava laughed.

"But why would you want to?" Missy exclaimed.

"In the past, we did have a rule about not creating anything that didn't already exist." Ava nodded as she flew slowly through the circle of fairies. "But it's not the rule now. I want you all to be creative, to imagine as big as you can. But just because you can imagine it, doesn't mean that you should create it. It's important to know your limits. As you do, your magic will increase and you will be able to create more and more things."

"Boring things." Bella muttered. What was the point of having magic if she couldn't create exactly what she wanted?

The world she saw around her was not the world that lived inside her head. Sure, the grove was beautiful. It was filled with flowers of endless colors. Plants and trees grew in every direction. There were woods to explore. Ponds, rivers, and lakes provided endless swimming options.

But Bella craved more than that. Seeing things so differently often made her feel a bit lonely.

Fifi gave her a light poke in her side. "Shh. Don't let Ava hear you fuss."

Bella pursed her lips, then stared down at the sand between her toes. She imagined that her toes were covered by bright orange fur. Long claws stretched out to dig into the sand. She grew and grew until she was bigger than the tallest tree in the grove. No one could tell her what to do or not to do then.

When she opened her eyes, she saw her tiny little toes with her tiny little toenails. She saw nothing but plain yellow sand covering her feet. She was as small and delicate as all the other fairies around her.

However, everyone seemed to be staring at her for some reason.

"Bella." Fifi's eyes widened. "What did you have for breakfast?"

"Huh?" Bella's cheeks grew hot.

"Was that your stomach growling?" Cara grinned. "Maybe you didn't eat enough!"

"Growling?" Bella pressed her hand against her stomach and giggled. "Sorry. It gets a little rumbly sometimes."

As the other fairies laughed with her, Bella glanced over at

Ava. She hoped that she hadn't noticed the growl. If she had, she didn't say a word about it.

"Alright, everyone." Ava clapped her hands and smiled. "Go out and create today!"

"Go out and create, huh?" Bella smiled at the thought.

She bolted off toward the tree house she claimed as her own.

"Bella! Cara and I are going to go for a swim. Do you want to come?" Fifi called after her.

"Thanks, but not today!" Bella waved over her shoulder.

She had some creating to do.

CHAPTER 3

Bella's tree house was tall and hollow. She figured it would be more than enough space for her project.

She grabbed a piece of fairy chalk—made from pressed fairy dust—and began to draw on the wall of the tree house. She smiled as the friend she imagined in her mind began to appear on the tree.

Once the outline was finished, she touched it and imagined it furry and orange. The fairy chalk glowed, then turned orange and then furry. She colored in the space within the outline. She added giant eyes, which she turned green, and a broad giant nose with a tiny tip. Then she drew in long teeth and big cat-like ears.

"Hi, JoJo!" She smiled at him.

She gasped as he smiled back. Was it just her imagination?

She touched the furry orange outline and didn't feel bark. Instead, she felt soft fur.

"Is this real?" Her eyes widened. She had created a few things, but she didn't think she had enough magic to create a creature like JoJo.

A low rumble filled her tree house.

She jumped at the sound. "What was that?" She looked into JoJo's eyes and heard the sound again. "Are you purring?" She smiled.

He smiled again.

She took a deep breath. If she could get him this far, why not see if she could take it a step farther? JoJo was harmless; he wouldn't be any trouble, and she could really use a friend that was just hers.

"It probably won't work anyway." She shrugged. "It can't hurt to try."

She placed her hands on JoJo's furry tummy. Then she closed her eyes. She took a deep breath and flapped her wings. They flapped faster and faster. She felt warm as her hands began to glow. Soon her whole body glowed. JoJo glowed too.

When she opened her eyes, she hoped she would see JoJo ready to give her a great big hug. Instead, she saw the outline she'd drawn. The fur was gone, the green eyes were gone, even the bright orange color was just the dull shade of fairy chalk.

"I knew it wouldn't work." She frowned.

A low rumble filled the tree house. Bella jumped at the sound, as it came from right behind her.

She spun around and slammed right into a pile of soft orange fur. It muffled her shriek of surprise.

"JoJo?" She stumbled back and looked up at the large creature. He was much bigger than she expected him to be.

"Bella!" He clapped his hands and stretched his arms out to her.

"Just as sweet as I imagined!" She smiled and hugged him the best she could. Her tiny body seemed even tinier when she snuggled up to him. "Oh, dear JoJo, you're too big for my tree house. What am I going to do?"

"Bella!" Fifi called from outside of the tree house. "Bella, are you in there? I heard something strange!" She pounded on the door.

"Oh no!" Bella gasped. "Fifi, I'm sick, stay out!" She coughed, then spread her body as wide as she could as the front door swung open. She knew her little frame did nothing to hide the giant orange creature behind her.

"You're sick? Oh dear, we'll have to get you some soup and —" Fifi stepped inside, then gasped. "Oh my, Bella! What did you do?" She jumped back so fast that she bumped into the wall behind her.

"Shh! You'll scare him." Bella stretched her arms wide as she stood in front of him. "He's shy."

"Shy?" Fifi's eyes widened. "How can anything that size be shy?"

"Isn't he beautiful?" Bella stroked the fur on his cheek and smiled. "Bright orange, just like I imagined."

"He's very b-beautiful." Fifi nodded as she inched along the wall. "I just hope he's not hungry."

"Don't be silly. His favorite food is strawberries." Bella picked one up from the bowl on the table beside her. "Here you go, JoJo."

The creature opened its large mouth and snatched the strawberry from her hand with his long teeth. "Good job!" She winked at JoJo.

"Bella, didn't you listen to Ava's lesson today?" Fifi shook her head. "I think this definitely falls under things you shouldn't have used magic to create."

"I listened! He's harmless. He is full of love." She tapped her fist against her chest. "I made him from my heart."

"Aw." Fifi fluttered up into the air and flew closer to the giant creature. "He is sort of cute."

"Very!" Bella grinned. "But I didn't expect him to be quite

so big." She peered up at him, then looked back at Fifi. "Please, you have to help me hide him."

"Hide him?" Fifi laughed. "You can't be serious. There's no way to hide a creature this size!"

"Fine." Bella narrowed her eyes. "You don't have to help me. I'll hide him myself. But you'd better not tell anyone about this, especially not Ava. If she finds out, she'll get rid of him for sure. I can't let that happen!"

"Wait, wait, don't be mad." Fifi sighed and sank back down to her feet. "I can tell that you really love him. I'll do my best to help you. But, if we're going to hide him, we can't do it alone. We're going to need some help. I'll find Cara. She'll know what to do. She always does!"

"What if she tells Ava?" Bella frowned and shook her head. "No, Fifi, it's too risky."

"She won't tell. Cara is our friend. She's very loyal. She'll do her best to help us." Fifi took Bella's hand. "I promise."

"Okay, I guess." Bella sighed. She wasn't so sure that Cara would help, but she had to find a way to keep JoJo safe.

CHAPTER 4

After Fifi left to find Cara, Bella turned to look at JoJo again.

"I guess I should have drawn you a little smaller." She stroked his fur. "But I think you're perfect."

"Bella!" JoJo clapped his hands. The movement shook the whole tree house.

"Don't do that!" Bella pressed her hands against his. "We have to be very quiet." She put her finger to her lips.

When she heard another knock at the door, she jumped.

"Fifi, is that you?" She flew toward the door and peered out the small peephole.

"No, it's me!" Missy sang out from the other side of the door. "I saw the tree shake and I thought you might need some help. Is there some kind of tree-shaking problem in the area?" She hopped up and down in front of the door. "Bella? Beeeel-laaaaaa?"

"I don't need any help, Missy!" Bella braced her back against the door to keep it closed. "I'm fine, thanks!"

"Are you sure? Why don't you just let me in? I've got nothing else to do. We can sing this new song I wrote. Bella?" She knocked on the door again.

JoJo shifted from one foot to the other.

"Shh!" Bella put her finger to her lips. "Maybe another time, Missy. I'm a little busy, bye!"

She held her breath and hoped that the helpful little fairy would take the hint.

When she heard her flutter off, she exhaled. "That was close."

Another knock at the door seconds later made her roll her eyes.

"Missy, I don't want to sing right now!"

"It's me!" Fifi poked her head through the door.

"And me!" Cara called out from behind Fifi.

"Okay, come in quick." Bella stepped away from the door.

"Oh my—what in the world—how did this—who did this?" Cara gulped. "Oh, Bella!"

"It's not a what, it's a who. This is JoJo." Bella frowned as she stroked the creature's orange fur. "I told you, Fifi, she's not going to help us."

"Of course I will." Cara crossed her arms. "We just have to figure out how to make him disappear."

"No!" Bella growled. "He's my friend! We just need somewhere to hide him."

"Oh." Cara looked way up at the top of JoJo's head. "Well, there's only one place in the grove that is big enough to hide him."

"Where?" Bella's eyes widened.

"Culpepper's Cave. It's this cave at the edge of the grove—in the mountain. Legend says that there once was a very shy fairy. She was so shy that she hid away in the cave and never came out. Her name was Culpepper. I don't know if it's true or not, but I know the cave is real." She blushed. "I was a little worried that Culpepper might still be in there, so I went searching once. But I never found her."

"How are we going to get him there, though? He's huge— and orange." Fifi pursed her lips.

"I can make him a special cloak. It won't last very long, but I can make him look like a tree." Bella rubbed her hands together.

"Wow, I never would have thought of that!" Cara nodded. "That should work. If anyone spots us, he can just freeze and no one will notice another tree in the grove."

"We need to get going." Fifi looked out through a small window. "When it's time for lunch, all of the fairies will be nearby. It will be harder to sneak him out if we wait much longer."

"I can do it!" Bella closed her eyes. She took a deep breath, then spread her hands wide. As her hands glowed, a material began to form between them. It grew larger and larger.

When she opened her eyes, she saw the large golden sheet. She tapped the center of the sheet, and bark began to spread out across the gold, followed by branches and bright green leaves.

"Oh, Bella, that's amazing!" Fifi clapped her hands.

"Will it fit?" Cara frowned.

"Let's find out." Bella threw the cloak over the top of JoJo's head.

He growled and squirmed.

"It's okay, JoJo." Bella took one of his clawed paws in hers. "I'll keep you safe."

"It's good enough." Cara nodded. "Let's go."

The three fairies led the cloaked creature through the grove.

They were almost to the cave when Ava swooped down from above them.

"What are you three up to?" She smiled at them. "Did you enchant a tree?"

Bella's throat went dry. Her heart pounded. Would Ava see JoJo under the cloak?

"We're just trying to be creative." Bella stammered. "We

thought it would be fun to see what it would be like for a tree to take a walk with us, instead of us walking through the trees."

"How interesting." Ava fluttered her wings. "Let me know what you discover. Just make sure you have him back in his usual place before dark, alright?"

"Absolutely!" Cara nodded.

"Will do." Fifi snapped her wings.

Bella nodded and kept her mouth shut tight.

Once Ava flew away, she gave JoJo a light push. "Hurry! Before she comes back."

Minutes later a silver mountain loomed up out of the tall trees of the grove. Beyond some bushes, Cara revealed the large opening to the cave.

"Here it is." She smiled. "Go on in, JoJo."

JoJo whimpered.

"It's okay." Bella pulled the cloak off him and it burst into tiny bits of fairy dust. "It's safe inside."

Bella watched as he crawled into the cave.

"Do you think it will be a good enough hiding place?" Bella lingered by the mouth of the cave. "I don't want to leave him here all alone."

"He'll be safe." Cara looked into her worried eyes. "I wouldn't leave him anywhere that wasn't safe."

"But how can you be so sure?" Bella peered back into the rocky opening of the cave. "What if he gets scared? Or lonely? What if he thinks I left him behind?" She wrung her hands. "I have to stay with him."

"Well, if you don't come back to the grove, everyone will know that something is up. Ava will send out a search party and they'll find you *and* JoJo. This is really the best way." Cara glanced up at the sun high in the middle of the sky. "It's already past lunch. We have to go before they come looking for us."

CHAPTER 5

"I'll be back, JoJo, I promise!" Bella blew him a kiss, then she flew off with Cara and Fifi.

All through lunch, Bella couldn't stop thinking about JoJo all alone in the cave. She wished she were there with him.

That night, as she tried to sleep, her heart ached at the thought of his being scared. She was scared too. What if something happened to him?

She gave up on sleeping and flew off through the grove to Culpepper's Cave.

"JoJo? Are you in there?" Bella peered into the mouth of the cave. Normally, she wasn't afraid of much, but the glow from inside the cave was eerie.

She heard the growl again and jumped back. "JoJo?" She whispered. "Are you hungry?"

Suddenly she heard feet pounding against the stone floor of the cave and they seemed to be headed straight for her. She gasped and jumped out of the way just before a bright orange blur burst free of the entrance. She landed on her bottom as she looked up at her friend.

Had he gotten bigger?

JoJo looked down at her and clapped his large paws.

"Bella!" He stretched his arms out to her.

"Aw, poor JoJo, did the cave get too small for you?" She flew up into his arms and nestled into his warm orange fur. He purred so loudly that Bella had to cover her ears. But she didn't mind. "I couldn't fall asleep because I was so worried about you." She sighed as she sank back down to her feet. She placed her hands on her hips and stared up at him. "Now, what are we going to do with you? You're bigger than the biggest cave. There's nowhere left to hide you."

"Bella sad?" JoJo sniffled, which made the leaves in the trees rustle loudly.

"It's okay, JoJo, it's not your fault." She bit into her bottom lip.

She hated to admit it, but she wondered if Ava might have been right. Maybe if she had a little more knowledge, she would be able to find a way to keep JoJo safe. She knew that if Ava found out about him, she would make him disappear.

Bella couldn't stand the thought of losing her friend. There was only one place left that she could think of to hide him.

Her heart pounded at the thought.

The forbidden place. Would he be safe there? Would the other creatures be kind to him?

She took one of his large claws in her tiny hand and looked into his eyes.

"JoJo, we have to find you a new home. It might be a little scary, but I will keep you safe. Okay?"

JoJo's big green eyes widened. He nodded and sniffled again.

Bella flew toward the forbidden place with JoJo plodding along behind her. Each step he took shook the ground. She tried to keep him on an open path, but he left behind many crushed bushes, broken trees, and even a flattened hill.

She continued to fly through thick branches, damp marshes, and darkness so deep that she had to glow to show their way. Eyes peered at them from bent trees and dark caves. Growls, chirps, and croaks alerted the rest of the forbidden place to their presence.

"Don't worry, JoJo, I'll keep you safe." Bella's voice shook a little as she spoke. They had traveled so far that her wings ached.

Finally, she spotted a large canyon. Its high walls would keep JoJo hidden from view and its width would give him plenty of room to roam. "Climb down, JoJo." Bella coaxed the giant creature.

"No!" JoJo growled and shied back from the edge of the canyon.

"It's okay. I won't let you get hurt." Bella tugged him forward, though she only managed to move the one claw she held.

"No, Bella!" JoJo sniffled and nearly swept Bella up his nostril.

"Ack!" Bella pushed her hands against the tip of his wide nose. "Careful, JoJo!"

"JoJo sorry." He sniffled again.

Bella narrowly escaped his other nostril by climbing up onto the bridge of his nose. From there she looked into his wide green eyes.

"I know you're scared, JoJo. I know it looks lonely down there, but I will come visit you every day. I promise. I need you to be safe until I can figure out a way to fix this." She stroked his furry orange cheek. "I'm going to, I promise. But if Ava or the other fairies find you, they won't understand you like I do. So for now, I need you to hide. Do you understand that, JoJo? Can you hide?"

"Hide." JoJo nodded, then blinked his big eyes. He bolted to the edge of the canyon, then jumped down inside.

Bella clung to his fur as he fell swiftly to the floor of the canyon.

JoJo landed on his feet.

Bella landed in his giant furry ear.

"Oof." She clung to his ear, too dizzy to fly.

After the dizziness faded, she looked up at the edge of the canyon. It seemed so far away and she was so very tired. JoJo's fur was soft and warm. Maybe if she had a quick nap, she would have enough energy to fly back to the grove.

She snuggled into the fur on the top of his head and soon fell fast asleep.

She opened her eyes again to the sound of a hawk calling high above her. She caught a glimpse of the sun through the thick clouds that gathered over the canyon.

"Oh no!" She jumped to her feet. "It's morning! JoJo, I have to go. But I'll be back!" She placed a quick kiss on the tip of his giant nose, then launched off into the air.

She flew as fast as she could back toward the grove. It was a long journey and she was exhausted by the time she reached her home.

The fairies were already gathered on the beach beside the stream.

She dove down to land, skidding to a stop a few feet away from Fifi and Cara.

"Bella, where have you been?" Fifi ran up to her. "When Cara and I saw you weren't here this morning, we went to the cave to look for you. But you weren't there and neither was JoJo! We were so worried!"

"What were you thinking, staying out of the grove all night?" Cara frowned as she crossed her arms. "We were just about to tell Ava to make a search party to look for you!"

"You didn't tell her about JoJo, did you?" Bella gasped.

CHAPTER 6

"No, we didn't, but we should have." Cara narrowed her eyes. "Did you sneak out and spend the night in that cave?"

"No, I didn't." Bella frowned. "He got bigger last night. I had to find a new place for him."

"Where?" Fifi grabbed her hand and led her away from the group. "How much bigger did he get?"

"A lot bigger." Bella winced. "I took him to the forbidden place, to a canyon. He fits just fine there. But he's so far away now." She ran her hands across her sore wings. "I flew back as fast as I could."

"I'm glad you're here." Ava walked over to them with her hands clasped behind her back. "We have a dire situation. It's quite terrible." She looked straight at Bella, then at Fifi and Cara. "Please join us. This is going to be a very important discussion."

"Yes, Ava." Cara smiled.

"We'll be right there." Fifi nodded quickly and grabbed Bella's hand.

As Ava fluttered away, Bella tried to pull her hand free of Fifi's. "I have to get out of here!"

"No, Bella, you can't take off now. If you do, Ava will know that something is wrong for sure." Fifi tightened her grip on Bella's hand.

"She already knows that something is wrong!" Bella groaned. "Didn't you see the way she looked at me?"

"She looked at all of us that way." Cara grabbed her other hand. "I don't think she knows, but we have to find out what she does know either way."

"Alright, fine." Bella's heart pounded as she joined the others at the edge of the stream.

Ava flew up into the air in front of them.

"I heard very strange noises yesterday and felt the ground shake a few times. So this morning I flew over the area and saw some very strange things. There were broken trees, smashed bushes, and even a crushed hill. I have no idea how something like this could happen." She took a deep breath, then sighed. "However, I suspect that it must have been caused by magic. I can't imagine anything that could cause this kind of damage that isn't magical. So our task today is to figure out what happened here." She spread her hands out to all the fairies. "I hope that if we all work together, we'll be able to figure out this mystery."

Bella clutched her hands together. She knew exactly how the trees had gotten broken and how the hill had been crushed. And she knew exactly where the trail would lead—right to JoJo! If all the fairies flew off looking for him, they were sure to find him. But would they really go into the forbidden place?

As the fairies gathered together, Ava began to assign them areas of the grove to search.

"I want you to look for any sign of magic use. Anything that is out of the ordinary. Please report it to me right away." She paused in front of Fifi, Cara, and Bella. "I'd like you three to fly with me."

"Sure!" Fifi offered a wide smile.

Cara grabbed Bella's hand and held tight. "Happy to join you." She smiled as well.

Bella smiled too. But she didn't have to force it. As long as she was with Ava, she could steer the elder fairy away from JoJo's hiding place. She flew into the air and stuck right by Ava's side.

As Bella looked down at all the broken trees and smashed plants, she realized that maybe JoJo hadn't been as harmless as she first thought. He didn't mean to cause any damage, but he was just too big to live in the grove. She wished there was a way that she could shrink him down to the size of a fairy, so that she could still have her friend.

"There!" Ava pointed ahead of them. "Do you see that huge footprint?"

"Oh, I don't think that's a footprint." Bella laughed. "But look over there." She pointed to a trail that led toward the other side of the grove. "Is that fairy dust I see?"

"Where?" Ava peered in the direction that Bella pointed. "I don't see any."

"Maybe it was just the sun sparkling." Bella zipped past Ava and headed in the opposite direction of the footprint. Yes, it was a footprint. It was one of JoJo's giant footprints.

Fifi swooped down beside her. "Bella, we can't keep this up all day. Ava is going to figure it out. Maybe it's time that we told her."

"She'll never understand, Fifi. She'll send JoJo away and she'll probably send me away too." Bella frowned. "I never meant for anything bad to happen. I didn't think that JoJo would hurt anything."

"He's just not meant to be in this world." Cara flew up on the other side of her. "There's no place that he fits!"

"There has to be." Bella snapped her wings. "I thought you

65

were going to help me, but you're not. I'll find a way to save JoJo, even if I have to do it by myself."

"But Bella, you don't have to!" Fifi called after her.

Bella ignored her friend. She flew as fast as she could. Only she knew where JoJo was and she planned to keep it that way. Her wings ached from how fast she'd flown earlier. She had to swoop and zip in all different directions to make sure that no one followed her.

By the time she reached the forbidden place, she was too tired to continue. She landed on a large slimy rock in the middle of a large swamp. Her feet slid in the muck and she landed with a grunt. It was no fun to sneak around all the time.

"Maybe Fifi and Cara are right—maybe I never should have created JoJo in the first place." She crossed her arms over her knees and tucked her face into her folded arms. If she weren't so exhausted, she might have flown right back to Ava and told her the truth. But at the moment, the last thing she wanted to do was fly.

When a tongue snapped past her, she jumped to her feet and shrieked.

CHAPTER 7

Bella turned around as the tongue flew right back past her.

"Hello there, little fly!" a large bullfrog croaked.

"I'm not a fly!" Bella jumped up into the air and tried to fly. Her tired wings only held her up for a few seconds.

"Tiny, winged creature equals delicious fly." The bullfrog snapped his tongue in her direction again.

"Stop!" She veered to the side just in time to avoid his tongue. "Fairies are protected, you're not allowed to eat them!"

"Nothing is protected here in the forbidden place." The bullfrog chuckled. "Now be still, I'm so very hungry."

"Never!" Bella gathered all her strength and flew high enough into the air to avoid the bullfrog's tongue.

She couldn't hover there forever. In the distance she heard another sound. A shout? She listened closely, then gasped as she recognized her own name.

"Bella!" Many different voices called her name. "Bella!" It sounded like the other fairies were on the hunt for her and they weren't far off.

"How kind of you to invite some friends." The bullfrog

rustled through the reeds at the edge of the swamp. "I have many friends too."

Suddenly several tongues snapped out from different areas of the swamp. Bella realized that the swamp was a trap, and the moment the other fairies flew into it, they would all be in great danger.

"Go back!" she shouted to the other fairies as they began to draw closer. "It's not safe! Go back!"

But the bullfrogs croaked as loud as they could to drown out her voice. Bella continued to hover, even as her wings ached. She knew if she tried to land, she'd be a bullfrog's lunch. She had to find a way to save her friends.

She took a deep breath and flapped her wings hard enough to get her high into the sky. She waved her hands frantically at the other fairies, while the bullfrogs continued to drown out her shouts.

Once she had their attention, she turned and flew as fast as she could toward the canyon. If she slowed down even for a second, those bullfrogs would surely catch up with her and the rest of the fairies too.

As she flew she had to dodge tongues that flew all around her. Soon the other fairies were dodging them too.

"Watch it!"

"Hey, stop that!"

Many of them shouted, while others whimpered in fear. Ava's voice carried above all of them and could even be heard over all the croaking.

"Be as calm as you can be, fairies. These bullfrogs aren't going to catch us. But you must keep flying!" Ava swooped to the side to avoid a bullfrog tongue.

Fifi and Cara flew side by side until a bullfrog tongue forced them apart in different directions.

Bella's heart raced as she watched the chaos unfold. Fairies zipped and dipped one way, then another way. The bullfrogs croaked louder each time they missed.

"Bella, we need to go back, not forward!" Ava cried out. "We're going deeper into the forbidden place! It's not safe here!"

"Don't stop!" Bella flew over to her. "The bullfrogs will never let us get back past them. We have to find a safe place where we can all land and rest."

"But where?" Ava spun in a circle before dodging another tongue. "There's swamp all around us."

"Maybe they'll get tired and leave us alone." Fifi peered down at the bullfrogs just as a tongue flew straight for her.

Bella bumped her out of the way before the bullfrog could have its snack.

"I don't think they're tired, just hungry." Cara gasped and ducked beneath the tip of another tongue.

"Why did you even come here?" Bella frowned. "It's not safe!"

"We were looking for you!" Cara placed her hands on her hips. "You flew off and disappeared. We were all very worried about you. We had to find out where you'd gone!"

"You should have just left me alone!" Bella sniffled. "Now we're all in trouble because of me."

"That's the part that you don't seem to understand, Bella." Fifi took her hand, just before she dodged another tongue. "You're not alone. Not anymore. You shouldn't ever feel like you have to be."

"This isn't your fault." Cara frowned. "We let all this get out of hand and we never should have."

"All of what?" Ava flew close to them. "Is there something I should know?"

Bella looked at Cara with pleading eyes. She could hardly

take a breath as she worried that Cara would reveal the truth to Ava.

"Ava, watch out!" Fifi tugged her out of the way of the snap of a tongue.

"Whew!" Ava gasped. "Thank you, Fifi, that was close!" She took a breath, then glanced at the others. "We'll talk about this later. Right now, we have to find a way out of here."

"I'm getting so tired!" Missy complained as she fluttered close to Ava. "Please, can't we rest?"

"I know, Missy, we're all getting tired." Ava pointed to a thin branch at the edge of the swamp. "If we can get to that branch, we can rest—for just a little while."

"It's too low." Bella shook her head. "The bullfrogs will be able to reach us."

"Maybe there?" Cara pointed to a large rock that jutted out from the soil at the edge of the swamp. "It's pretty high."

"Good eye, Cara!" Ava nodded. "Fairies!" She snapped her wings to get their attention. "To the rock!" She pointed to it.

"That's not going to work!" Bella cried out, but the other fairies eagerly flew toward the rock.

CHAPTER 8

"Please! Follow me!" Bella waved her hands at the other fairies. "The bullfrogs are just behind us. They are determined to catch us. They will find a way up onto the rock! If we rest, they will snatch us up!"

"Why did you lead us here?" one of the other fairies shouted. "You've put us all in danger!"

"I didn't mean to." Bella hung her head. "I'm so sorry."

"You should be!" another fairy piped up from the back of the crowd. "Now we're all trapped here, thanks to you!"

"Stop!" Cara flew in front of Bella and faced the rest of the crowd of fairies. "Bella didn't do anything wrong. She was trying to help her friend, just like we are. Fighting isn't going to save us. If we're going to escape the bullfrogs, we're going to have to work together."

"Cara's right." Fifi called out. "We need a really good idea. We need to imagine a way out of this before it's too late. Don't waste your energy on being mad or placing blame. Think of a solution instead!"

"And I know just the fairy to do it!" Ava swooped down in front of Bella. "It's you, Bella!"

"Me?" She stared at Ava.

"Of course you." Ava looked into her eyes. "You're the most imaginative fairy I know. I'm sure you have the idea that will save us all."

"But my ideas are the reason that we're here in the first place." Bella shook her head. "I don't think another idea will help at all."

"Just try." Ava hovered closer to her. "You're our only hope. You and your big imagination. How are we going to get away from those bullfrogs?"

"I don't know!" Bella huffed. Then suddenly her eyes widened. She remembered the way the ground shook when JoJo walked. Maybe, if he could stomp his feet, it would shake the swamp enough to knock the bullfrogs into the water. She could imagine the large waves that JoJo's stomping could create.

She had to go get him in order to help her friends.

But if they see him, they'll want to get rid of him, she thought.

Even though she loved JoJo very much, she knew bringing him out of his hiding place was the only way to help the other fairies.

"Fifi, I have to go," she whispered. "I'll be back. I'll be back with the solution to our problem. Just tell the other fairies to keep flying. I'll be back as soon as I can."

"Bella, you shouldn't go, it's not safe!" Fifi flew up into the air to try to catch her.

But Bella was already headed for the edge of the swamp.

She couldn't let her friends suffer because she had done something foolish. If only she had truly listened to Ava's words when she'd talked about how to use magic, maybe none of them would be in this position.

Instead, she had insisted on doing things her own way.

Now she wasn't sure that she would be able to save them at all, but she knew that she had to try.

As she swooped out of the way of a bullfrog that flicked his tongue at her, she knew that her tired wings wouldn't carry her very far. The canyon was looming closer, but she wasn't sure that she'd be able to reach it. With the bullfrog still just behind her, she knew that he wouldn't give up easily.

Ahead of her, there was a thick gnarled branch that hung low, close to the ground. She couldn't fly over it, as thick spiky vines wrapped around it and created a wall with the next highest branch. She was too tired to try to fly any higher.

Her only option was to fly under it. Which would put her right in the bullfrog's range.

She trembled with fear as she swooped down below the branch. She heard the bullfrog leap behind her. Just as she reached the lowest point, she spotted a hollow log on the ground. It looked too narrow for the bullfrog to fit.

She sank all the way to the ground and dove into the log just as the bullfrog flicked out its tongue. The sudden snap created a breeze that tickled Bella's feet as she scrambled further into the log. She hurried forward into the thick darkness, less afraid of it than she was of the bullfrog behind her.

As she crept forward, her hands sank into a sticky mess and her wings tangled in something. She took a deep breath and used her magic to make her hands glow.

Once she did, she wished she hadn't.

There were spiders all over the top of the inside of the log. Spiders about her size and spiders far bigger. One of the largest spiders began to crawl toward her.

Bella squeaked with fear as the spider came closer and closer. Then it waved its long front legs toward her.

CHAPTER 9

"Please don't hurt me!" Bella whispered. "My friends need my help. If I don't get back to them, all the fairies in Sunflower Grove will be bullfrog snacks."

"Oh, those bullfrogs! They are always hunting us when we leave our home." The spider snarled. She waved her feet again. "Don't be frightened, little fairy. I won't hurt you. I want to help you. I have a way for you to get away from the bullfrogs safely. It's how we leave our log. Follow me." The spider crawled toward the end of the log.

Bella wasn't sure whether to trust her. Was her offer of help just a trick?

When she looked back at the other end of the log, she heard a loud croak. She knew she didn't have much choice but to follow the spider.

She wiped off some of the spider webs from her wings and crawled after the spider. As she did, she heard a loud thump. The log suddenly shook.

She gulped as she realized that the bullfrog had jumped on top of the log. He planned to beat her to the end of it and be waiting there for her when she reached it.

The spider paused at the end of the log. She began to weave a long web.

As Bella watched, the spider crept forward under the web and continued to weave it until it reached a tall tree on the outside of the swamp. Then she scuttled quickly back to the log.

She looked at Bella. "The bullfrogs don't like the taste of our webs. They can break through it eventually, but you should have enough time to get to that big tree. Then you can climb up out of the bullfrog's reach. But you must be quick!" She gave the fairy a light shove with her two front legs.

"Thank you!" Bella waved to the spider as she bolted off under the web.

She was halfway to the tree when the bullfrog slammed its tongue into the web canopy.

Bella gasped and ducked down.

The bullfrog groaned. "Ack! Gross!" He wiped at his tongue and coughed.

Bella took the chance to run even faster toward the tree.

The bullfrog slammed his tongue into the web again. "That is disgusting!" he complained and wiped his tongue on the ground. "Nastiest thing I've ever tasted!"

Bella reached the tree and bolted up the bark. As tired as she was, she couldn't move as fast as she would have liked.

She heard the bullfrog leap behind her.

"You'll be back, little fairy! I know that you won't leave your friends all alone. I'll be waiting!" he croaked at her, then chuckled.

Bella ignored him and raced up the tree. She reached a long branch and ran across it. Then she jumped to the next branch. She used her wings to flutter, but she couldn't quite fly.

She jumped and hovered from branch to branch until she neared the edged of the canyon. She was so relieved to see it that she flew up into the air. But her wings were too sore and tired to hold her up.

Instead, they folded on her back and Bella began to fall into the canyon.

She landed on soft warm fur and heard a familiar voice.

"Bella!" JoJo cradled her in his large paw and smiled.

"JoJo." She clung to his fur and sighed with relief. "I'm so happy to see you." She looked up into his big green eyes. "I need your help, JoJo. I have to save my friends." She reached up and stroked his cheek. "But it's going to mean that we have to say goodbye."

"Goodbye?" JoJo's eyes grew big.

"Yes, I'm sorry." Bella frowned. "But there's no other choice. Will you help me?"

JoJo nodded and smiled again. "Help Bella!"

"I knew you would. You're such a good friend, JoJo." She directed him back toward the swamp.

As she clung to his orange fur, he carried her easily over all the dangers she had encountered. He didn't even notice the bullfrog or the log full of spiders. He didn't seem the least bit concerned about the spiky vines or the mucky swamp.

"There!" JoJo pointed to the cloud of fairies that still hovered together, surrounded by bullfrogs. They all looked exhausted. The bullfrogs continued to snap their tongues as they edged closer to the fairies.

"JoJo, will you dance with me?" Bella looked into his eyes.

"Dance?" JoJo grinned.

"Like this." Bella began to stomp and jump in his outstretched paw. She stomped as hard as she could, then jumped as high as she could.

"Dance." JoJo nodded. He stomped as hard as he could, then jumped as high as he could.

Bella clung to the fur on his paw as she flew through the air with his movements. The ground shook and the swamp water sloshed. The bullfrogs and the fairies all looked at JoJo.

"What is that?" one of the fairies shrieked.

"A monster!" another cried out.

"Fly away!" a third hollered.

"No, no! Don't fly away!" Cara hovered in front of the other fairies. "He's here to help us."

"He's Bella's friend!" Fifi added. "He won't hurt any of us!"

"Bella's friend?" Ava swooped down in front of Cara and Fifi. Then she turned her attention to the giant orange creature that continued to stomp and jump at the edge of the swamp.

The bullfrogs clung to their perches, but the lily pads and slimy rocks they clung to were too slick. As the ground shook and the water sloshed, they slid right off.

"Hurry!" Bella called out to them. "Fly to JoJo! He will keep us safe!"

The other fairies hid behind their wings and each other, too frightened to fly to safety.

CHAPTER 10

"Please!" Bella cried out. "He won't hurt you, I promise!"

"She's right!" Fifi called out. "He's very sweet. Follow us!"

Cara flew toward JoJo. Missy followed after her. So did Fifi. Then Ava zipped toward him and landed right on the top of his head.

"Let's go, fairies!" Ava snapped her wings. "If Bella says he is to be trusted, then he is to be trusted!"

The other fairies flew toward JoJo and nestled into his fur.

Ava peered down at Bella, who climbed up JoJo's fur to his shoulder.

"It seems like you have a lot to tell me, Bella. It's a good thing we have a long journey back to the grove." She crossed her arms.

"I'm sorry, Ava." Bella sniffled as she looked up at her. "I did something very wrong and I put us all in danger. I never meant to. I let my imagination run away with me."

"You created this creature?" Ava slid down the side of JoJo's neck and settled on his shoulder beside Bella.

"I did." Bella nodded.

"We knew about it too." Cara sighed as she and Fifi landed

on JoJo's shoulder as well. "We should have told you right away. But we wanted to help Bella."

"Why did you create him, Bella?" Ava looked into her eyes.

"I just wanted a friend." Bella frowned.

"But you have friends." Fifi looked at Bella. "We're all your friends."

"Sometimes it doesn't feel like it." Bella hung her head. "When you and Cara are together, you forget all about me."

"Oh dear." Cara frowned. "I'm sorry, Bella. Fifi and I have been friends for so long and sometimes I forget that you are new to the grove."

"I'm sorry too, Bella." Fifi hugged her. "I never want you to think that I'm not your friend. I'll try harder to make sure that you know how important you are to me."

"To all of us." Ava put her hand on Bella's shoulder.

"Important?" Bella shook her head. "More like I'm dangerous to everyone. Look what I've done."

"Yes, look what you've done." Ava patted JoJo's shoulder. "Never in all my dreams have I imagined a creature as wonderful as this."

"But he has no place here. He's too big." Bella sighed and clasped her hands together. "I know that you'll have to make him disappear, Ava. He doesn't belong in Sunflower Grove." She looked up as they reached the edge of the grove. "If he tries to walk through there, he'll crush more plants, bushes, and even hills."

"Alright, everyone!" Ava snapped her wings. "Off to rest, all of you!"

Missy started to fly away with the other fairies, then she swooped back.

"Ava, it's not all Bella's fault. It's mine too."

"Yours?" Bella looked at her with surprise.

"What do you mean, Missy?" Ava looked at the young fairy.

"I knew about JoJo too. I saw him in Bella's tree house. I followed them when they hid him in the cave. I wanted to help. So I went into the cave and tried to use my magic to make him smaller. But it didn't work. He got bigger instead." She sniffled. "I'm sorry, Bella, I was really only trying to be your friend."

"That was the glow I saw!" Bella gasped. "Missy, it's okay. It's not your fault. I'm the one that started all this."

"Alright, girls, it's time to give JoJo some space." Ava waved them off of the gentle giant.

Bella hugged his neck, then looked up into his big green eyes. "Thank you so much for being such a good friend, JoJo."

"Help Bella." JoJo smiled as she fluttered away from him.

Cara and Fifi hugged Bella as Ava turned toward JoJo.

"You saved us all today, my new, beautiful friend. Thank you." She held up her hands. They began to glow. Then the glow spread over her whole body. As she placed her hands on JoJo, he began to shrink. He shrank until he was only a little bigger than the fairy that stood in front of him.

Bella held back tears as she waited for him to disappear.

"That should do it!" Ava brushed fairy dust off her hands.

"What?" Bella's eyes widened.

"I meant it when I said that I want all of you to be creative. We need some changes around here. Every fairy in Sunflower Grove has a special gift to offer that is much more important than magic. Today you used that special gift, Bella. You were able to imagine ways to protect your friend and ways to rescue all of us. I could never have created JoJo with my imagination. You see the world in a very special way, Bella. Thanks to your big imagination, our grove now has a new guardian. We are tiny creatures and even though we have magic, sometimes that's not enough to protect us from the much larger beasts that roam. Having a giant proved to be quite helpful today, don't you think?" Ava smiled. "Now JoJo can be big or small, as he chooses."

"Really?" Bella gasped. "Oh, Ava, thank you!" She flung her arms around the elder fairy.

As Ava hugged her back, Bella realized that there was a place in Sunflower Grove for everyone, even the largest of creatures with spiky orange fur.

BOOK 3: CARA

CHAPTER 1

Cara leaped from one long yellow petal to another. The petal bowed beneath her feet and almost bent. She waved her arms through the air to steady herself, then fluttered her wings to help catch her balance.

"That's cheating!" Another tiny fairy landed on a petal beside her. "I saw you flutter your wings. No wings, remember?"

"I was going to fall!" Cara huffed, then laughed. "But you're right, it is cheating. I don't know how you're so good at this, Devi."

"Practice." Devi grinned as she dusted off her dress. "The pollen can make a bit of a cloud sometimes, so I know to hold my breath. There's a certain spot on the petal that is the best place to land." She looked back up at Cara. "But it's different on every petal. You have to know how to find it."

"Clearly I don't." Cara shook her head and smiled. "But it sure is a lot of fun."

"If you keep practicing, you'll get it, Cara. All it takes is a little bit of patience. Watch." Devi leapt from the petal she was on to the next one and landed right in the center of it. Her wings were still folded; her feet didn't slide a bit.

"That's amazing, Devi. You really have a talent." Cara shrugged. "I just don't think I'm designed for graceful things. I'm always bumping into things, and when the other fairies dance, I can't seem to keep up."

"Maybe that's because you're always busy looking out for someone else." Devi jumped back to the petal that Cara stood on.

"Maybe." Cara smiled. "Which reminds me, I promised Fifi I would help her with her garden. Maybe we can try this again tomorrow?"

"Sure, I'll be here." Devi waved to her as Cara flew away.

Cara soared over Sunflower Grove. She looked down at all the other fairies. Some were in their gardens. Others splashed in the crystal blue stream that flowed through the grove. Her heart filled with warmth as the sight of her many friends.

As she flew down toward Fifi's garden, she laughed at the sight of her trying to drag a large bag of seeds. The bag was almost as big as Fifi and she tumbled backward when she tried to tug it.

"What are you going to do with all those seeds?" Cara landed right beside her.

"Plant them, of course." Fifi laughed.

"Why not just do it the way we always do?" Cara ran her fingers through the seeds in the bag. "They're not heavy if you just use magic to lift them."

"I know, I know." Fifi tried to catch her breath. "But ever since I planted a seed the old-fashioned way, I've fallen in love with gardening. I like taking the time to tend to them, making sure that they're planted in just the right places, with just enough space to grow. It's harder than using magic, but it's fun."

"If you say so." Cara smiled. "Let me help you with the bag."

Together they tugged the bag of seeds further into the garden.

"It'll only take a few hours for me to plant all these. We can go for a buzz over the stream after that, if you'd like." Fifi wiped some dirt off of her forehead.

"Maybe you should go for a swim instead." Cara laughed. "It looks like you could use a bath."

"Ha, ha!" Fifi tipped her head back and forth and put her hands on her hips. "I'll have you know, I don't mind getting a little dirty. We can't all be as picture perfect as you, Cara." She fluffed her hair and pursed her lips.

"Picture perfect?" Cara laughed so hard she buckled over. "Okay, tell me another one."

"Please, you might not see it, but the rest of us do." Fifi gave her a big hug. "There, now you're as dirty as me."

"Great." Cara brushed some soil off her dress and rolled her eyes. "I guess that means that I'm the coolest fairy in all the grove."

"I don't know about the coolest." Fifi laughed. "But you're definitely the dirtiest."

"I might need to fix that." Cara scooped up some soft soil from the ground and flung it at Fifi.

"Hey!" Fifi flew up into the air to avoid the dirt. "Oh, that's it! It's war!" She grabbed two handfuls of soil and flung each one back at Cara.

Cara gasped and ducked down behind the bag of seeds. She jumped back up when she had her hands full of soil. The battle continued until a sharp snap of wings made them both freeze.

"Just what is going on here?" Ava, the elder fairy of the grove, sank down to the ground.

"Gardening?" Fifi gulped as a clump of dirt fell out of her hair.

"Oh yes, we were planting seeds." Cara cleared her throat and dropped the dirt that she had packed her hand with.

"Hard at work, how nice." Ava folded her arms and smiled. "This bag of seeds looks pretty full, though, and the two of you look pretty dirty. It's almost time for lunch. You two had better get cleaned up." She eyed Cara for a moment. "What are you hiding behind your back?"

"Nothing, Ava." Cara smiled sweetly.

"Interesting." She pointed her finger at Cara. "I'm watching you, little fairy."

"Nothing to see here." Cara smiled even wider.

"Get cleaned up!" Ava flew off as she laughed.

The moment the elder fairy turned her back, Cara spun around and flung the dirt that she'd been hiding at Fifi.

"You naughty fairy!" Fifi shrieked as she scooped up two more handfuls.

"Well, if we have to take a bath, we might as well get extra dirty!" Cara laughed. "Race you to the stream!"

She darted off toward the stream with Fifi on her heels.

CHAPTER 2

There were many things that Cara loved about the grove. She loved the beauty, the colors, and the wide sky that stretched across it. But most of all she loved her friends. There wasn't a single fairy in all of Sunflower Grove that she didn't enjoy spending time with.

As she splashed into the water, she accidentally knocked Bella off of the lily pad she was floating on.

"Ah!" Bella crashed into the water, then popped back out. She clung onto the lily pad as she gasped for air between coughs.

"Bella, you shouldn't open your mouth under the water." Cara frowned. "Are you okay?"

"I wouldn't have opened my mouth if I hadn't been screaming when you knocked me off my lily pad!" Bella glared at her. "Didn't you see me?"

"I'm sorry, I thought I had plenty of room." Cara glanced up at the bright sun. "You shouldn't be lying out in the sun like that anyway. You'll get a sunburn!"

"Thanks." Bella rolled her eyes, then swam off to the edge of the stream.

"I think I upset her again." Cara winced as she swam over to Fifi.

"Oh, you know Bella, she gets lost in her head sometimes and doesn't like to be interrupted. It's that big imagination of hers." Fifi smiled. "Don't worry about it. She'll be over it by dinner."

"I hope so." Cara swam down under the water to get all the dirt out of her hair. When she popped back out, she noticed the youngest fairy, Missy, wading into the water. "Missy, where's your acorn?" Cara swam toward her.

"I'm fine, I'm not going that deep." Missy smiled.

"Until you can swim you shouldn't be anywhere near the water without your acorn." Cara crossed her arms. The younger fairies used the acorns to keep them afloat until their wings were developed enough to help them swim.

"I don't want to have to lug it around. I'm staying in the shallow part of the stream." Missy placed her hands on her hips.

"No way, Missy. You could get knocked over and swept up in the current. You shouldn't be in the water without your acorn." She pointed to the edge of the stream. "Go get one, then you can come back in."

"You know you're not an elder fairy, Cara!" Missy glared at her. "You're just a regular fairy like me. You don't get to tell me what to do!"

"Missy!" Fifi swam over to her and Cara. "Why are you shouting?"

"She won't let me swim!" Missy pointed her finger straight at Cara. "She always thinks she can tell me what to do. I'm not getting out of the water!" Missy splashed her hands against the water, which sent water spraying straight at Cara.

"Missy!" Cara splashed her back. "I'm just trying to keep you safe. Why would you want to risk drowning?"

"Okay, okay, that's enough." Fifi swam between them. "I

think Missy is just trying out a little freedom, Cara. Don't worry, I'll stay with her and make sure that she's safe."

"It's the rule." Cara sighed. "Everyone knows the rules."

Missy stuck her tongue out at Cara, then waded off through the water with Fifi at her side.

Cara swam to the other side of the stream and climbed out. She squeezed the water out of her hair and tried not to think about Missy's attitude. She knew not all the fairies liked her and sometimes it made her really sad. She wanted to be friends with everyone, but it didn't always work.

She started to walk back toward her tree house, when she realized she'd left her pouch on the other side of the stream. She decided to hop across a few rocks instead of getting wet again.

She did her best to hop the way that Devi had taught her, but she still slid and almost landed right in the water. She swooped up into the air just before she did. As she hovered over the stream behind a bush, she heard voices.

"I can't stand it anymore," Missy complained.

"Me either," Bella groaned.

"You two are being silly," Fifi whispered. "Cara is our friend."

"She thinks she's in charge of everything and everyone!" Missy stomped one foot.

"She *is* very bossy," Bella muttered. "Don't breathe underwater, Bella. As if I don't know that. Don't lie out in the sun, Bella. I mean, who does she think she is?"

"If I want to wade in the water, I should be able to," Missy snapped. "She shouldn't tell me not to. I can't do anything without her watching."

Cara's heart sank as she heard the other fairies talk about her. She knew they didn't always like her, but it sounded as if they hated her.

Her eyes filled with tears.

"Maybe Cara can be a stickler sometimes, but she's always there to help solve any problem. She is a very loyal friend." Fifi sighed.

Cara's heart sank even farther. Even Fifi thought she was bossy? Her best friend?

Tears spilled down her cheeks. She'd never felt so sad before.

She knew if she flew any higher they would see her. She tried to hop back across the rocks again instead. As she landed on the last one, she slid, stumbled, and then splashed into the water.

When she broke through the surface, all three fairies were staring at her.

"Cara! I thought you had gone off to lunch." Fifi smiled at her.

"I forgot my pouch." Cara looked down at the water.

"Oh, let me get that for you!" Missy scooped it up and flew it over to Cara.

"Thanks." Cara took the pouch without looking at her. She tried hard not to start crying again.

"No problem, I love to help." Missy flew off.

"Do you want to walk with me to lunch, Cara?" Fifi flew over to her.

"No. I need to dry off." She flew away before Fifi could look into her eyes.

CHAPTER 3

Cara flew as high as she could. She didn't want anyone to be able to see her.

As the wind dried her wings and dress, she thought about what she'd heard her friends say. Maybe they were right. Maybe she was a little too quick to tell people what they should and shouldn't do. But it was only because she wanted to keep them safe.

She loved everyone so much that she looked for any danger that might befall them. If she saw it, she could prevent it from happening.

But now that she'd heard what her friends really had to say about her when she wasn't listening, she thought perhaps she could change it. Yes, it hurt her feelings, but that didn't mean that they were wrong.

She paced around her tree house for some time, thinking about how to fix the problem.

"From now on, I won't tell the other fairies what to do. I won't give them advice, even if I think it's what's best for them. I can be a good friend, I know I can."

She flew out of her tree house and headed for the mushroom palace to share lunch with her friends.

When she arrived, she tried to be more cheerful. But the sight of Missy and Bella reminded her of what they really thought about her. She decided to sit at a different table.

When Devi waved her over, she smiled and joined her.

Cara's plate was full of moss, herbs, and delicious shoots, but she only took a nibble.

"Aren't you hungry?" Devi leaned close to her and pointed to her wooden plate. "You haven't eaten a bite."

"I did eat one." Cara smiled. "But no, I'm not very hungry."

"Wow. I'm starving! After all the leaping we did this morning, I really worked up an appetite." Devi scooped up a big handful of moss and flower petals and opened her mouth wide.

Cara opened her mouth to warn her not to eat so much at once—that she could choke—but instead, she closed her mouth again.

Devi crammed the food into her mouth, then began to cough. She grabbed her shell full of water and took a drink. Then she cleared her throat. "Oops, sorry, I guess that was a little too much."

"It's okay if you're okay." Cara smiled.

"I am." Devi took another sip. "Which is a good thing because I have big plans for tonight."

"Tonight?" Cara leaned closer. "What are you up to? More leaping?"

"No, not more leaping." She laughed, then raised an eyebrow. "Can you keep a secret?"

"Of course." Cara nodded and leaned even closer so that Devi could whisper to her.

"I've been planning an adventure. I've been studying the stars at night. I think the way they are arranged might be some kind of message. They move around so much that it's taken me a long time to figure out how to track them." She shook her head. "I wanted to give up more than once, trust me."

"That's amazing, Devi! I'd love to learn more about the stars. But what does that have to do with tonight?" Cara smiled.

"I'm going to go out flying tonight. I finally figured out the perfect spot for me to view the shift in the stars. It's high enough to get a clear view, but hidden enough that I won't get into trouble. I hope." She held up crossed fingers. "I know it's against the rules to go out flying at night, but I've been working so hard to figure this out. I just have to do it. You won't tell, will you, Cara?"

Cara took a deep breath. She fought back the words that she wanted to say. She wanted to warn Devi that flying at night was never safe, that at least she should take someone with her. She wanted to insist that Devi tell Ava. She wanted to advise her that Ava would probably figure out a way to help her with her adventure. But she didn't. She just forced her lips into a tight smile and shook her head.

"No, of course I won't tell. I said I would keep the secret, right?" She took another breath. "But it sounds like so much fun. Would you like to have some company? I'd be happy to go with you."

"Oh, that's nice of you, Cara. I really do appreciate it. But..." She shook her head back and forth and scrunched up her nose. "I'm not sure that this would be your kind of thing."

Cara's heart dropped as she stared at Devi. She probably didn't want her to go. Why would she? If all the other fairies thought she was bossy, then Devi probably did too. Why would she want a bossy fairy with her on such an important adventure?

She looked away quickly as tears flooded her eyes. "I understand."

"Next time, Cara. I promise." Devi gave her a quick hug, then picked up her empty plate and flew away from the table.

Cara stared down at her still uneaten food. She still wanted to warn Devi not to go out on her own. But she was too busy with her own broken heart to even consider it.

"I guess I have to try harder." She looked up at all the other fairies laughing and eating together. She wanted to be part of that. But as long as she was the bossy fairy, she would always be left out.

CHAPTER 4

When it was time for dinner, Cara decided not to go. She curled up in her bed instead. She still didn't feel very hungry anyway. She kept thinking about earlier in the day when she'd overheard her friends by the stream.

She wanted to be a better friend, but she was also hurt.

Why couldn't they like her for who she was? She certainly didn't mean to be bossy. She just wanted everyone to be safe. Didn't that make her a great friend?

At some point, she fell asleep.

She woke the next morning to a rumbling tummy. She opened her eyes and felt hungrier than she had ever felt before. She flew over to the window in her tree house and peeked out.

The sun had just risen. The breakfast bell began to ring. Her stomach rumbled again. She didn't have any food stashed away in her tree house.

But going to the mushroom palace would mean that she had to face her friends. She wasn't sure that she wanted to do that. Maybe she could wait until everyone was done with breakfast and then sneak inside for whatever was left.

She flew out of her tree house toward the mushroom palace.

Instead of going inside, she hovered beneath one of the large mushroom caps and watched as all the other fairies gathered. There was Bella, followed by Fifi and then Missy. They laughed and hugged each other. No one seemed to notice that Cara wasn't there. Maybe they were relieved.

Cara sniffled and hid in the shadow of the mushroom cap. As the other fairies arrived for breakfast, she watched for Devi. She wondered how her nighttime flight had gone and what she might have learned about the stars. She wasn't sure if she would work up the nerve to ask her, but she did want to know.

Fairy after fairy flew into the mushroom palace. Soon even all of the elder fairies had come inside. But she didn't see Devi. Maybe she had missed her.

Curious, she flew closer to the dining room. She peeked between mushroom stalks for any sign of Devi. All the other fairies were there, but Devi was not.

Cara's heart began to pound. What if Devi hadn't come back from her flight the night before?

She forgot all about her hungry tummy and flew straight for Devi's tree house. She knocked on the leaf door.

"Devi, are you in there? It's me, Cara! I just want to know if you're okay!" She waited a moment but didn't hear an answer.

Cara started to open the door. Then she stopped. Was this what her friends didn't like? Was it wrong for her to open Devi's door to make sure she was okay? What if Devi just wanted to be left alone?

She waited a second longer, then opened the door. She had to know that her friend was safe.

As she stepped inside, she saw right away that Devi's bed of dried leaves, soft moss, and fluffy flower petals hadn't been slept in.

"Oh no! She didn't come home last night!" Cara's heart

pounded. "Maybe she's still out flying. Maybe she stayed out all night. Maybe she was just a little late for breakfast."

She flew back to the mushroom palace. All the other fairies were just about done with their breakfast. She flew into the dining room and searched for any sign of Devi.

"Cara! There you are!" Fifi stood up from the table. "You weren't at dinner last night and Devi said that you didn't eat your lunch. Are you sick?"

"It doesn't matter. Have you seen Devi this morning?" Cara looked straight into Fifi's eyes.

"Cara, what's wrong?" Fifi's face grew pale. "Are you okay?"

"Just tell me Fifi! Have you seen her?" Cara's voice grew louder as she began to panic.

"No, I'm sorry, Cara. I haven't seen her." Fifi frowned. "I understand if you wanted to eat breakfast with her instead of me."

"It's not that." Cara's eyes filled with tears. "I've done something terrible. Something absolutely horrible. I can't believe I let this happen!"

"It can't be that bad." Fifi hugged her tight. "You always look out for everyone. I'm sure whatever it is, it's not your fault."

"You're wrong, Fifi." Cara pulled away from her and wiped at her eyes. "It's all my fault! I have to find Ava."

"Wait, why don't you let me help you?" Fifi grabbed her hand. "Tell me what's wrong."

"No, there's no time. I have to find Ava right now!" Cara flew up into the air. "Ava! Ava, where are you?"

"Cara?" Ava swooped in from the higher mushroom caps. "What's wrong, my dear?" She hovered right in front of her. "You look so frightened."

"Ava, I'm so sorry. I know I will be in trouble for not telling you and I don't care. I just need your help to find her, please!" Cara could hardly speak as tears flowed down her cheeks.

The other fairies all began to gather close.

"Cara, I can help." Missy flew up to her. "Just tell us what's wrong. We'll all help."

"It's Devi." Cara took a deep breath and tried to speak clearly. "She's missing. She hasn't been home. I checked her tree house. She wasn't at breakfast. I knew it was a bad idea when she told me. I really did. But I didn't stop her. I should have told you right away, Ava. Now she's missing and it's all my fault."

"Slow down, Cara." Ava took her hands and looked into her eyes. "You need to tell me everything. Start from the beginning."

Cara looked toward Fifi, Missy, and Bella. She knew why she hadn't told Ava about Devi's plans. But she wasn't ready for her friends to know that she heard them talking about how bossy she was.

"Devi has been studying the stars. She went for a night flight last night. All by herself." She bit into her bottom lip as she looked back at Ava. She could only imagine how upset the elder fairy would be.

CHAPTER 5

"You knew and you didn't tell me?" Ava's eyes widened. "Why not, Cara?"

"I just..." She took a deep breath, then frowned. "Devi asked me to keep it a secret and I didn't want to tell her what to do."

"I see." Ava's eyes narrowed. Then she snapped her wings. "We need to form a search party. First, we'll search the grove, then if we haven't found her, we'll go further. Cara, did she tell you where she might be going?"

"She said it was a place that was high enough to see the stars, but still hidden." She lowered her eyes. "I offered to go with her, but she didn't want me to."

"Try not to worry too much, Cara. We'll find her." Ava wrapped her arm around Cara's shoulder.

"I should have told you." Cara sniffled.

"That doesn't matter right now. What matters right now is finding Devi. She could be lost or she could have gotten herself into some kind of trouble. The younger fairies will stay here and look all through the tree houses and the mushroom palace. Make sure you look everywhere. The older fairies will join me on a wider search." She gestured to a few of the older fairies. "Please, gather some supplies in case Devi is injured."

"I'll come with you, Ava." Cara flew up into the air. "I can get the supplies."

"No, Cara. I want you to stay here. Make sure that everyone is safe and that you look everywhere. She could be hiding for some reason." Ava sighed. "I wish she had just come to me."

"Ava, please, I can't just stay here. Please let me come with you. I know that I didn't do the right thing, but I can make up for it." She hovered close to Ava.

"No, Cara." Ava spoke in a stern voice. "I don't want to risk anyone else getting lost. The elder fairies know the grove and all its unique places far better than the younger fairies. Now, start the search." She jumped up into the air and flew off toward the edge of the grove.

"Are you okay, Cara?" Fifi took her hand. "We can search together if you want."

"No." Cara placed her hands on her hips. "I'm going to look for Devi. I know she's not here. She's out there all alone somewhere because of me."

"No, it isn't your fault. Devi made that choice. You even offered to go with her." Fifi shook her head. "She knows better than to fly off alone."

"Why would she want to go anywhere with me?" Cara frowned, then flew higher in the air. "You and Missy can handle the search. I'm going to find Devi."

"I'll come with you!" Fifi zipped up beside her.

"It's okay, Fifi. I'll stick close to the elder fairies. I'll be fine. You're needed more here. Missy loves to help, but she can't do it all on her own. I'll be back—with Devi." She waved to Fifi, then flew as fast as she could.

She wanted to catch up with the elder fairies before they got too far ahead of her. As she recalled what Devi had told her about the place she planned to visit, she searched for areas that were wide open with a good view of the sky.

"But she also said she'd be hidden from view." Suddenly Cara had an idea. "The waterfall!"

She snapped her fingers, then flew off away from the elder fairies and away from Sunflower Grove. She knew she shouldn't be flying on her own outside of the grove, but she hoped that her hunch was right. If it was, she wouldn't be flying home alone.

She crossed the stream, then a large lake. She flew partway up a large mountain until she came to the base of a large waterfall. She looked up at the water as it crashed over the ridge of the mountain. It splashed into a small pool at the bottom which fed into the stream that eventually ran through Sunflower Grove.

It seemed to be the perfect place for Devi to study stars. It was high and the mountain was clear of any vegetation that might block her view.

Cara flew up the side of the mountain until she reached the very top. As soon as she landed on one of the slippery rocks that jutted out from the water, she could see all the danger. If Devi had perched on the same rock, she might have slipped. If she had slipped, she would have landed in the rushing water and crashed down to the bottom of the waterfall with it. With wet wings, she wouldn't have been able to fly up before she went over the edge of the waterfall.

Cara did her best to keep herself steady on the rock. She knew better than to stand on it, but she hoped that Devi might have left some kind of sign behind—anything that would prove that she'd been there.

A sparkle in the water caught her eye. She leaned close to see if it might be a clump of fairy dust. Before she could see what it was, a gust of wind pushed her right off the slippery rock.

As the cold water rushed over her, Cara squeezed her

mouth shut tight. She knew if she swallowed any water, she would have a hard time getting back to the surface.

She thrashed her hands through the water in search of anything that she could grab. Her fingers curled around the edge of a leaf. She managed to pull herself up on top of it just before she reached the edge of the waterfall. Cara caught sight of the big drop from the top of the waterfall right as the leaf tipped over the edge.

She gasped, then closed her eyes tight. In her mind she imagined a safe cozy pile of leaves at the bottom of the waterfall to land in.

But she knew that what was actually beneath her was an icy cold pool dotted with large rocks.

CHAPTER 6

Falling felt a lot like flying to Cara, only far more terrifying. She clung as tightly as she could to the leaf as it kept her afloat on the journey down the waterfall.

When she crashed into the water below, the force jolted her entire body. She gritted her teeth and did her best to stay upright on the leaf as the water swirled around her. The icy splashes that hit her in the face left her sputtering and shivering.

She breathed a sigh of relief as the leaf drifted into calmer water. Exhausted, she collapsed on the leaf and closed her eyes. She felt the warm sun on her skin. She took a few deep breaths to calm herself, then she opened her eyes.

As she looked down into the water, she saw the same sparkle she'd seen at the top of the waterfall. It wasn't evidence of Devi's being there. It was just the sparkle of gemstones at the bottom of the water.

Cara wasn't sure whether to be disappointed or relieved.

She shook off her wings until they were dry enough for her to fly. Then she jumped up into the air.

She knew it wasn't safe to walk on those slippery rocks, but she'd still done it. It was a mistake she never would have made in the past.

"You have to be more careful, Cara." She flew up into the air and spread her wings wide.

As the sun dried the last of the water on them, her worry grew. What if no one was able to figure out where Devi had gone? Maybe if she had just followed her without her knowing, she would have been able to help her, or at least tell the others where she was.

She blinked back tears and flew faster.

"Devi, where are you?"

She swooped through a thick group of vines and ducked under a large wasp's nest.

Had Devi flown through the same spot? Had she known not to touch the vines in case one turned out to be a snake? Had she known not to bump into the wasp's nest?

Cara could have told her all these things if she'd been with her.

Exhausted, she sat down on a long branch that overlooked the stream. She could see for many miles. There were hills and valleys and great big meadows.

She didn't think Devi would be in any of those places. So where could she be?

She lifted her eyes higher in search of the highest place that she could find. Her eyes settled on the tallest tree in Sunflower Grove. It was also the oldest.

The elder fairies considered it a special place, but they warned the other fairies that it was only safe to look at. As old as it was, it wasn't very sturdy and there were concerns about its falling one day soon.

Cara often steered other fairies away from it when they were tempted to use it to see how high they could fly.

The truth was, no fairy could fly to the very top. It didn't have enough branches to rest on. If a fairy tried, her wings would tire before she even got close.

"She can't be up there." Cara narrowed her eyes. "Could she be up there?"

She stood up on the long branch and continued to stare at the tree. It was the perfect spot for Devi to see the stars and she could easily hide in the thick leaves at the top of it. It seemed crazy to even consider it, but her instincts told her that Devi might have found a way. Devi was a very determined fairy, who took the time to figure things out and often found new ways of looking at things.

Cara flew over to the tree and landed at the bottom of it. She walked around its wide trunk. On the ground there were several leaves and nuts, but no sign of Devi's being there.

She peered up at the low branches. She spotted something dangling from one of them. Her heart skipped a beat. Could it be?

She flew up to the branch and landed right beside the strap of a pouch. She picked up the strap and ran her fingers over it. Yes, it was just like the strap on her own pouch. Only the pouch wasn't there.

Had Devi gotten it tangled and ripped it free? Had she fallen and tried to grab onto it?

Cara's stomach twisted at the thought.

She flew back down to the ground and searched through the leaves just to be sure. If Devi had fallen, she wasn't there anymore. Maybe she had already gone back to the grove?

Cara looked around for any of the elder fairies. They would know what to do. But she didn't see anyone in any direction.

She looked way up at the top of the tree. If Devi was up there, then she was in danger. Cara couldn't just fly away without trying to check for her. She decided to fly up to the highest branch she could get to.

It took some time for her to reach it. By the time she landed on it, her wings were limp and sore. There was still a lot of tree before the top.

"There's no way Devi made it up there on her own." Cara drew a deep breath and frowned. Had she wasted time by investigating the tree?

She stretched out on the branch and let her wings rest. She closed her eyes and wished that she could send a message to Devi. "I'm going to find you, Devi. Help is coming."

"Watch out!" A high-pitched voice squeaked as claws skittered across bark.

CHAPTER 7

"What?" Cara jumped to her feet just in time to see large beady eyes and a bushy tail headed straight for her. She flew up into the air with what strength her wings had left.

The squirrel slid underneath her across the branch. He clung to the very end of it as his body slid off. Then he flipped his legs up and scrambled until he was safely on the branch.

"Sorry, I was going too fast!" he panted as he shook his fluffy tail. "I didn't expect anyone to be on this tree. No one ever is and now all of a sudden, two little fairies show up."

"Two?" Cara landed on the branch again and clung to the trunk of the tree. "Have you seen another fairy?"

"Why, yes. Just last night." He crept toward Cara. "What are you doing up here? Fairies aren't allowed here."

"I came to look for my friend—the fairy that you saw last night. She's missing." Cara stared into his eyes. "Do you know where she is?"

"She told me it was a secret." The squirrel flicked his bushy tail. "I am very good at keeping secrets."

"I'm worried about her. She was supposed to come home

and she hasn't. I'm afraid she might be hurt." Cara looked into the squirrel's eyes. "She's my friend. She would want me to know where she is."

"You think she would. But she told me it was a secret! Why would she go up there all alone if she didn't want to be left alone?" The squirrel shook his tail at Cara. "I think you're trying to trick me."

"I'm not, I promise." Cara crept closer to the squirrel. "I need to find her. She has many friends that are worried about her. Will you please tell me where she is?"

"I took her to the top of the tree." The squirrel looked up. "At least as far as I could go. She's probably still up there." He looked back at Cara. "I can take you if you want. But you have to hold on tight."

"I will." Cara nodded quickly.

"Climb onto my back." The squirrel turned his back to her.

Cara started to climb up, but the squirrel's bushy tail got in her way. She gave it a light push.

"Watch the tail!" he huffed and swished it across her face.

"Sorry!" she sputtered as she dodged the tail. She climbed up onto his back and sunk her fingers into his fur.

"Here we go!" the squirrel yelled and launched up the tree.

Cara clung to the squirrel's fur as she bounced up and down on his back. He moved faster than she knew a squirrel could. Minutes later, he skidded to a stop.

Cara looked down at the ground and could barely see it. Her mind spun as she realized how high they were.

"Is this where she is?" Cara slid down off the squirrel's back and perched on a tiny wedge of a branch beside him.

"No, but this is as far as I go. If I go any higher, the hawks can snatch me. I told the little fairy she shouldn't go any higher either, but she did. She flew right up there." He pointed his tail toward the very top of the tree. "If the hawks haven't gotten her, that's where she'll be."

"How terrible." Cara gulped. What if the hawks had snatched Devi?

All the creatures in the grove agreed not to harm the fairies in exchange for their nurturing the nature around them with their magic. But a hawk might not realize that a fairy was a fairy before it was too late. The fairies knew the dangers of hawks and always made sure to stay out of their hunting grounds.

"I have to go up there and make sure that she's safe."

"I wouldn't do it if I were you." The squirrel spun around and fluffed his tail in her direction. "Good luck, little fairy!" He bolted down the tree trunk so fast that he sent pieces of bark flying into the air.

Cara shivered as she looked up at the very top of the tree. She could fly the short distance to it, but it was still scary.

She took a deep breath and reminded herself that her friend was up there. She would do anything to protect Devi.

She jumped into the air, then began to flap her wings. At first, she wobbled a little in the wind. It seemed colder and stronger than it had down below. She found her balance and began to fly upward.

At the top of the tree were a few branches and many leaves. She landed on one of the highest branches and glanced around. All she saw were leaves.

Her heart dropped as she realized the mistake she'd made. The squirrel had left her behind and there was no way she could fly all the way down to the next branch from the top of the tree. Her heart pounded with fear. Worst of all, there was no sign of Devi. It had all been for nothing yet again.

"Devi! Where are you?" she shouted at the sky above her.

"Cara?" Devi's muffled voice called out.

"Devi?" Cara froze. "Is that you?" She could hear her, but she couldn't see her.

One of the leaves began to rustle. Then Devi poked her head out from under it.

"Devi!" Cara gasped, then rushed toward the tiny fairy.

CHAPTER 8

"Cara!" Devi cried out. "I can't believe you found me! I didn't think anyone would come. No one knew where I was." She pushed the leaf off to the side. "The hawks were circling this morning, so I hid."

"Devi, you poor thing." Cara crouched down beside her. "Why did you stay here all night?"

"I didn't mean to." She grabbed her leg and pointed to her ankle. "I'm stuck!" She grabbed at the two thick branches that pinned her ankle. "I've been trying to get free, but I just can't do it."

"It's alright, I'm here now." Cara smiled at her as she crouched down to look at her ankle. "How did this happen?"

"I fell asleep last night when I was looking at the stars. When I woke up everything was slippery with dew. I tried to stand up and my foot slipped and somehow it got wedged in there." She sighed. "I've been trying to pull it out just a little bit at a time, but I haven't been able to get it free." She wiped at her tear-stained cheeks. "I almost gave up. Cara, I'm so glad that you're here."

"I wouldn't have gotten here if it wasn't for your squirrel

friend." Cara wiggled her eyebrows as she laughed. "I've never ridden on a squirrel before." She hoped to brighten Devi's mood.

"Oh!" Devi laughed too. "Me either. It was bumpy, wasn't it?"

"Sure was. I'm still a little dizzy from it." She put her hands on Devi's shoulders. "I'm here now. Don't worry, we'll get you home. Let's take a look at that leg." She crept closer and eyed Devi's ankle. "Yes, that's a pretty tight spot."

"I know. And it hurts." Devi bit into her bottom lip. "I thought it was just stuck, but now I think it might be worse. It seems like it's swollen."

"Yes, it does." Cara's heart skipped a beat. If Devi's foot had swollen, it would be very hard to get it out of the tight spot. She pushed her worry aside and did her best to tug at Devi's foot.

"Ow! Oh, that hurts so much!" Devi shrieked. "Cara, please stop!"

"I'm sorry, Devi." Cara pulled her hands away as she frowned. "Maybe I can use some magic to get the tree branches apart."

"No, don't!" Devi waved her hands in the air. "I tried that this morning and the entire tree shook. I thought it was going to topple! I was so scared."

"That's a good point." Cara frowned. "The magic probably traveled all the way down to its roots. That's why the elder fairies tell us not to come to this tree."

"I know." Devi closed her eyes. "But it was the exact perfect spot to get the answer I was looking for, and I've been working on this sky map for so long."

"Sky map?" Cara raised an eyebrow.

"It's there." She pointed to a rolled-up piece of paper. "I finished it last night. I'm not sure if it was worth it now."

"A map of the stars?" Cara's eyes widened. "All of them?"

"As many as I could see." She nodded as she rubbed her leg. "And it also shows where they will be in the sky and when. I worked really hard on it."

"Devi, that is amazing." Cara smiled, but she wondered why Devi hadn't told her more about what her plans had been. Was it because she thought Cara would tell her not to do it? "Maybe we could try rubbing some fairy dust on your foot. It might make it slippery enough to get it out."

"It's worth a try." Devi sighed. "I lost my pouch on my way up the tree. It got stuck on one of the branches and the strap ripped off. Then my pouch fell."

"It's alright, I have mine." Cara opened up her pouch and pulled out a handful of fairy dust. "I'll try to be gentle." She rubbed some of the powder on Devi's foot."

"Oh no!" Devi winced.

"I'm sorry, did I press too hard?" Cara frowned.

"No, it's not that. Look up!" She pointed to the sky.

Two big hawks were flying in a slow circle around the top of the tree.

"Hawks!" Cara gasped. "We have to stay calm and still. If we don't move, they might not see us."

"I think it's too late for that. Get under here!" Devi grabbed Cara's arm and pulled her under the large leaf. "If they can't see us, they won't dive."

Cara scrunched down beside Devi and tried to be still, but she shivered as she heard the hawks crying out above them.

CHAPTER 9

"I'm so sorry, Cara." Devi whispered.

"Shh! Don't move." Cara snuggled closer to her friend. She wished there was a way she could protect her from the hawks. Then she recalled the fairy dust in her pouch. "I have an idea."

"What is it?" Devi looked into her eyes.

"Just stay under here. No matter what. Got it?" Cara stared back at her.

"Don't go out there! They'll see you!" Devi gasped.

"That's what I'm hoping for." Cara slid out from under the leaf. She climbed over the other leaves until she was in full view of the hawks. "Hungry?" She fluttered her wings and jumped up and down. "Yes, you! I'm talking to you!" She waved her hands in the air.

The hawks began to circle faster. She reached into her pouch and filled her hands with fairy dust. She knew that she would only have one chance. She also knew that her idea might not work. But she thought it was the only way to keep Devi safe.

"Hey, you two big buzzards! Yes, that's right, I called you buzzards! Come and get me!" She flew up a few inches from the leaf. The sun sparkled on her wings.

The hawks began to dive.

Cara's heart raced as she watched the massive creatures draw closer. What if her plan didn't work?

She held her breath and waited until the hawks were close enough that she could see their eyes. Then she flung the fairy dust at their faces. The cloud of fairy dust billowed between her and the birds. The hawks cried out and flapped their wings.

As the dust cleared, she saw that they had turned to fly away. The fairy dust in their eyes was enough to deter them from any prey that might be in the tree.

"Yes!" She jumped up and down as the hawks disappeared in the distance. "It's okay, Devi, they're gone!"

"Thank goodness!" Devi pushed the leaf aside. "What did you do?"

"I just gave them an eyeful of fairy dust." Cara smiled. Then her smile faded. "But we don't have long. They might come back. Let me take another look at your foot." She reached down and tried to pull it free. After several tugs and Devi's crying out in pain, she sat back on the branch and frowned.

"That's it." Devi sighed. "I'll never get free. Cara, you should go before the hawks come back." Devi pulled the leaf back over her. "There's no reason for us both to be in danger."

"No, I'm not going to leave you. We'll figure something out." Cara took her hand. "I'm so sorry that I didn't tell you not to do this when you told me about it. I just didn't want to be bossy."

"Bossy?" Devi pulled the leaf back off her face. "What do you mean?"

"I heard Fifi and some of the other fairies talking about me. They said I was very bossy and they didn't like it." She frowned. "I guess that's why you didn't want me to come with you last night."

"What?" She peered at her. "You think I didn't want you to come because I thought you were bossy?"

"Yes. Why else would you want to go off by yourself?" Cara shook her head. "I know you know better than to do that."

"It's not that at all. I don't think you're bossy. You know a lot of things and you give great advice, but this was supposed to be a secret. I wanted to surprise everyone in Sunflower Grove when I finished it. I didn't want anyone else to go with me, because I didn't want anyone else to know the secret." She closed her eyes. "It was such a bad choice."

"We all make mistakes, Devi." Cara hugged her. "Don't feel bad. I should have told Ava what you told me. Then she would have stopped you from coming up here. But I didn't want you to be mad at me."

"Oh, Cara, I would never be mad at you for being a good friend to me." She hugged Cara back. Then she gasped. "Oh no! The hawk is back!"

"Get under the leaf." Cara swung the leaf over Devi, but there wasn't time for her to get under.

She crouched down low as the hawk drew closer and closer. She reached into her pouch to get more fairy dust. Her fingertips rubbed along the bottom of the pouch. She had used it all up!

As the hawk got closer, she ducked behind one of the twigs that shot off the branch. She knew it was too late not to be seen, but she didn't want to make it easy for the hawk to grab her.

The hawk swooped down so low that Cara could see its long feathers. Her eyes widened and suddenly she jumped out from behind the twig.

"Help!" She waved her hands in the air as the hawk hovered close and shouted as loud as she could. "We need help here! Please help us!"

The hawk cried out. The bird was so close that the sound hurt Cara's ears and his breath stirred her hair.

CHAPTER 10

"Cara!" Ava waved from the back of the hawk. "Oh, Cara, what are you doing here?" She and two other elder fairies clung to the feathers near the hawk's neck. "When the other hawks said that there was a fairy on the top of this tree, I thought it would be Devi."

"Devi is here too!" Cara called out. The moment that she'd seen Ava perched on the back of the hawk, she knew that they would be saved. Tears of relief flooded her eyes. "Devi, come out. It's safe!"

"It is?" Devi pushed the leaf aside. "But I heard the hawk so close. Ah!" She jerked back at the sight of the large creature.

"It's okay. This is Pana. She's a friend. She flew us up here, as we couldn't get up here ourselves." Ava glanced over at the other two elder fairies. "We found her, Jana."

"Just in time too." Jana narrowed her eyes. "What a pair of foolish fairies you both are."

"This is not the time to discuss that." Ava shook her head. "Devi, is your foot stuck?"

"Yes, it is." Devi sniffled. "I can't get it free."

"Zari, can you help?" Ava flew down from the hawk's back to the branch.

"Yes, I can." Zari and Jana flew down to the branch as well.

"I've tried pulling it free, but it won't work." Cara frowned.

"You were supposed to stay at the grove." Ava met her eyes.

"I know." Cara took a step back. "But I just couldn't. I needed to make sure that Devi was okay."

"And she wasn't." Jana shook her head. "It isn't safe to go off on your own, Devi."

"I know."

Cara and Devi watched as Zari rubbed her hands together. They began to glow, but instead of gold, they turned a bright orange color.

"I won't do it again. I promise," said Devi.

"Good." Zari grabbed Devi's leg, then took a deep breath in.

As the other fairies watched, Devi's ankle and foot grew smaller and smaller until her leg popped free of the branches, then returned to normal size.

"Wow!" Devi gazed at the elder fairy. "How did you do that?"

"Fairies who don't follow the rules don't get to learn higher magic." Jana crossed her arms.

"One day you'll find out, Devi." Ava wrapped her arms around her. "Does it hurt terribly?"

"Some." Devi forced a smile. "I'm just happy to be free."

"Let's go." Ava helped them both up onto Pana's back. "It's time we all went home."

As they flew through the sky, Cara nestled close to the bird's feathers. She was relieved that Devi was safe, but she wasn't sure if she was ready to face her friends.

Pana swooped down over the grove but didn't land.

"We can fly down from here." Ava smiled and patted the top of the bird's head. "Thank you for your help, my friend."

The bird nodded her head.

Once all the fairies were off her back, she flew across the sky.

Cara stared after her. She recalled how frightened she'd been when she'd first seen the hawk. If it hadn't been for Pana's help, she and Devi might still be on the top of that tree.

Cara helped Devi fly down to the ground. When they landed, the other fairies rushed forward to surround them.

After many happy cheers, Fifi stepped forward. "Cara, I knew you would find her." She clapped her hands. "You're such a good friend!"

"Am I?" Cara looked back at her. "I wasn't sure that you thought so." She felt her face go warm.

"What do you mean?" Fifi frowned. "Of course I think so. Everyone does."

"Not everyone." Cara glanced over at Bella and Missy. "At least that's not what you said yesterday by the stream."

Fifi's eyes widened. She clasped her hands together and frowned. "Oh, Cara, I didn't know that you heard that. I'm so sorry." She looked over at Bella and Missy. "I wish you would have told us." She looked back at Cara. "We all love you very much. Sometimes we say things that we shouldn't just because we're mad or upset."

"She's right." Bella stepped forward and met Cara's eyes. "Cara, sometimes it seems like you're always telling me what to do, but you're also always the first person who has great advice to give. Whenever I'm having trouble with anything, you stick by me and help me figure it out. I'm sorry I said those things."

"Me too." Missy stepped forward beside Bella. "Sometimes I want to do everything myself. I like to be the one that helps people, not the one that needs help. But you were right. I shouldn't have been in the water without my acorn. You were just trying to keep me safe because that's what a good friend you are. We are so lucky to have you." Missy threw her arms around Cara and gave her a big hug.

"So you see, Cara, your friends need you." Ava wrapped an arm around her shoulders. "You have a very special gift that you offer all of us. It's the gift of loyal friendship. Being a good friend doesn't mean always being nice. Sometimes it means telling your friend the truth, that something she is doing could hurt her. Sometimes it even means telling an elder fairy when you think your friend is in trouble, even if you think it will upset her."

"That's what I should have done." Cara sighed. "Then Devi never would have been in danger."

"You are a wonderful friend, Cara. Devi should have told me what she was up to." Ava looked over at Devi. "I would have helped you to do what you wanted to do, Devi. It's okay to have secrets, but if it's a secret that could get you hurt, then it's not a good secret. I and the other elder fairies are always here to help you."

"I know that now." Devi frowned. "I'm sorry that I didn't think things through."

"You put yourself in grave danger." Jana pointed her finger at Devi. "And as for you..." She turned her attention on Cara. "I thought you were wise enough to make good decisions. But clearly, you still have a lot to learn."

"And learning is the most important thing you can do." Ava put her hand on Jana's shoulder. "They are young fairies, Jana. They have much to learn. The important thing is that you do better from now on. I'm sure you will, won't you, Cara? Devi?" She looked between them both.

"Absolutely." Cara nodded.

"I promise." Devi looked at all the fairies and then at Cara. "You risked your life to save me, Cara. But you shouldn't have had to. I won't make the same mistake again."

"I'm so happy you're safe." Cara hugged her tight.

"All that matters is that we're all safe now and we're all friends." Ava clapped her hands. "I think this calls for a special celebration. Tonight we'll all get together on the ridge for some hot honey and berries. Then Devi can show us her special surprise. Does that sound good, Devi?"

"It sounds perfect." Devi smiled. "Cara, will you help me get ready for it? I could really use a friend." She held her hand out to her.

"Absolutely!" Cara grinned.

Together they flew off into the sky. Cara knew now that it was okay for her to always want to look out for her friends, but it was always good to talk to them about how they felt. She always wanted to be the best friend that she could be. She hoped that one day she would be as wise as Ava and that perhaps she could learn the higher magic that had allowed Zari to save Devi.

Ava was right. There were so many things for her and her young fairy friends to learn, and Cara couldn't wait to discover each one of them.

BOOK 4: DEVI

CHAPTER 1

Devi's wings hummed as she hovered over the pile of rocks beside the slope of the mountain at the edge of Sunflower Grove. The rocks were quite large for a small fairy to move, but she picked one up just the same and carefully flew it over to a wide open flat section of the grove.

Exhausted from the first trip, she perched on the rock and shook out her wings.

"Phew." She wiped a few drops of sweat from her forehead, then she launched into the air again.

As she flew back to the pile of rocks, another fairy swooped down beside her.

"Good morning, Devi!" Missy fluttered her wings.

"Good morning, Missy." Devi smiled at her but focused on the next large rock she needed to pick up.

"What are you doing?" Missy watched as Devi tried to pick up the rock.

"I'm working on a special project." Devi smiled as she managed to get the rock off the ground.

"Let me help you with that!" Missy grinned. She waved her finger through the air, then snapped her wings. A sprinkle of fairy dust landed on the rock. An instant later, it sprouted wings and began to hover in the air.

"No thank you, Missy!" Devi frowned as she stared at the rock. "Now I can't use it!"

"Why not?" Missy flew over to the rock. "It will go wherever you tell it."

"Go into the stream!" Devi gave the rock a light shove in the direction of the stream.

The rock wobbled, fluttered its wings, then crashed into the stream that wound through the trees of the grove.

"Missy, I really need to take my time and do this right. It takes a lot of patience, but it will be worth it."

"I was just trying to help." Missy sank to the ground. "Maybe if you tell me what you're doing, I can help you more."

"You'll find out soon enough." Devi flashed her a smile.

"You're going to be finished in time for the trip though, right? The flight to the top of the mountain?" Missy walked around the pile of rocks. She kicked a few pebbles as she did.

"Yes, I'll be finished by then." Devi picked up another large rock. "Let me get back to work and I'll surely be done in time."

"Okay." Missy jumped up into the air and flew off.

Devi's arms ached as she carried the next rock over to the flat area. Her wings protested when she flapped them.

"One rock at a time, Devi. Just be patient, you'll get it done."

She smiled at the thought of the trip to the top of the mountain. They only did it once a year and it was a very important event. After they reached the top, they would celebrate with special songs and dances. And the food—she licked her lips at the thought—the food was always good.

She fluttered back over to her pile of rocks and prepared to pick another one up.

"Hi there, Devi!" Fifi landed on top of the pile. "What are you doing?"

"It's a special project." Devi looked up at her. "Careful on those rocks, please."

"Sure thing." Fifi fluttered down to the ground. "It looks like a lot of work." Fifi tilted her head to the side as she watched Devi struggle to pick up one of the rocks. "Why not just use your fairy dust to move the whole pile?"

"For this task, I need to take my time." Devi gulped as the weight of the rock nearly knocked her backwards.

"Careful!" Fifi lunged behind Devi and gave her a firm push to keep her from falling over.

"Thanks." Devi sighed. "I've got to pay attention to what I'm doing, Fifi."

"Okay, I understand." Fifi fluttered off, glancing over her shoulder as Devi half-flew and half-stumbled over to the flat stretch of grass.

Devi dropped the rock onto the ground, then winced as it rolled out of place.

She sighed as she looked at the rock.

"That's not where you're supposed to be." She crouched down and gave the rock a hard shove to get it into place.

"Let me help you with that." Cara landed beside her and pushed the rock alongside her.

"Thanks, Cara." Devi smiled as she brushed the dirt off the top of the rock.

"It would be a lot easier if you used magic to help you." Cara took a step back and looked over at the pile of rocks near the foot of the mountain. "Are you planning to move all of these rocks?"

"Yes." Devi took a deep breath and rested her hands on her hips. "It's going to be quite a job."

"A little bit of magic can help you get it done." Cara rubbed her hands together and began to flutter her wings.

"No, Cara!" Devi stepped in front of the rocks. "I know that you want to help, but I can't let you do this. Please don't use any magic."

"Devi, it's not wise—or safe—to lift all these rocks. You could pull a muscle or break a bone or even drop one on your foot." Cara met her eyes. "It's foolish to think that you can do all this. Your arms and wings will be exhausted."

"I know what I'm doing, Cara." Devi crossed her arms as she looked at her friend. "Please, just let me work. I need to get this done before we fly up to the top of the mountain. I have to stay focused."

"Devi, listen to me, you're never going to get this done before then. Why don't you take my advice and just use a little bit of magic?" Cara frowned as she put her hand on Devi's shoulder. "It'll be much faster and you won't have to work so hard."

"I don't mind the work." Devi gave Cara's hand a light pat, then fluttered off to the pile of rocks. She picked up the next rock, hovered for a moment, then flew over to the flat patch of grass.

CHAPTER 2

By the time the sun began to set, Devi's arms hurt. In fact, everything hurt.

She sat down on the pile of rocks she still needed to move and sighed. Her project was only half-finished.

"Maybe Cara was right, maybe I'll never be done on time." She frowned, then took a deep breath. "It's okay, I'll just keep working. As long as I stick to it, I'm sure it will get done."

The dinner bell rang, but Devi remained by her pile of rocks. She picked up another one and flew it over to the others.

It was a hard job, there was no question about it.

She imagined how much easier it would be if she just used her magic. Fairy dust could help in so many ways. She still had so much more to learn about it, but what she did know was enough to help her—only not with this task. For this task, she needed a different kind of magic.

As she picked up another rock, she heard a soft voice right beside her.

"You've been working so hard all day."

"Who said that?" She glanced around. All she saw were rocks.

"Me." A tiny caterpillar lifted its head to look up at her from one of the rocks in the pile. "I've been watching you work so hard."

"Hi there." Devi smiled as she crouched down to peer at the little caterpillar. It was green with purple spots and had little spikes that jutted up out of its back. "I don't think I know you."

"I'm Pearl." The caterpillar inched closer to her. "Aren't you tired?"

"Very." Devi perched on the rocks beside Pearl. "But if I take too long a break, I might not get this done in time."

"You still have to rest." The caterpillar crawled onto the back of Devi's hand. "It's important."

"It is." Devi's stomach rumbled. "I suppose I should eat too."

"That is very important." The caterpillar nodded her head. "Don't worry, I'll keep an eye on your rocks while you're gone."

"Thank you, Pearl." She lightly tapped the top of the caterpillar's head with her fingertip. "I'll be back soon."

She jumped off the rocks and flew toward the Mushroom Palace. It was where all of the fairies gathered to eat.

She arrived a few minutes late. All the tables were surrounded by fairies enjoying their food.

Devi settled into a seat beside Fifi.

"Devi, we thought you might not be coming." Fifi took a big sip of nectar from a large yellow flower.

"Ava just went looking for you." Cara nodded as she looked at Devi. "How is your project going?"

"It's getting there." Devi frowned. She didn't want to tell them that she wasn't sure if she would get it done on time.

"I know it's a surprise, but I'm so curious to find out what it will be." Cara sighed.

"I'd like to hear about it too." Ava stepped up behind Devi and smiled. "I've heard about all your hard work."

"You have?" Devi smiled up at Ava.

"Yes. I do hope that you're giving yourself some time to rest." She plucked a bit of grass from Devi's hair.

"I'm taking a break right now." Devi nodded.

"Good. Are you looking forward to our trip up the mountain?"

"Yes, I am." Devi clasped her hands together under the table. Would Ava be able to tell that she wasn't telling the whole truth? How could she look forward to the trip that she wasn't sure she would be able to go on?

"Good. If you need any help with anything, please do let me know." Ava patted the top of Devi's head, then flew off to another table.

"Wow, you have Ava curious too." Fifi grinned. "You won't give us even a little hint?"

"No, I'm sorry." Devi stood up from the table. "In fact I should get back to work."

"But you barely ate!" Cara called out to her.

"I ate enough." Devi waved to her friends, then flew out of the Mushroom Palace.

She had to get her project finished. There was no time for breaks.

As she picked up another rock, she thought about the journey up the mountain. It was a spectacular experience that she didn't want to miss.

"Hi again." The caterpillar climbed over one of the biggest rocks.

"Hi, Pearl." Devi smiled and picked up another rock.

"Are you making a circle?" The caterpillar walked around in a circle on the top of the rock.

"A big one." Devi nodded. She placed the rock next to the last one she'd put down in the grass.

As she turned back to get another one, Pearl gasped.

"Wow! That was fast!"

"What was fast?" Devi tipped her head to the side.

"The circle!"

Devi spun around and found the circle of rocks was complete. She stared at it for a moment, then she put her hands on her hips.

"Alright! Who did this? Come out now!" She tapped one foot against the ground.

"Hi." Missy fluttered down from a nearby branch. "You're very welcome." She smiled as she snapped her wings.

"No, Missy." Devi sighed. "I am not going to thank you. This is something I have to do on my own." She rubbed her hands together and fluttered her wings. As her hands began to glow, she held them out toward the rocks that had been added to the circle.

The rocks floated up in the air, then crashed to the ground in a pile away from the circle.

"Devi!" Missy crossed her arms. "I used a lot of fairy dust to do that."

"I'm sorry, Missy, I know you're just trying to help, but you're only making things worse. I have to stay focused if I'm going to get this done." She looked straight into Missy's eyes. "Please don't help me anymore!"

"I'm sorry, Devi." Missy sniffled as she fluttered off.

"Poor Missy." Pearl sniffled too.

"I know I wasn't nice, but this has to get done!" Devi huffed as she picked up another rock.

CHAPTER 3

The moon climbed higher in the sky as Devi continued her work. When the stars began to glitter, she sat down on the ground to rest. She was worn out but happy that she almost had the circle complete. As long as she kept moving, she guessed she would have her project done before the trip up the mountain. All she had to do was close her eyes for just a moment.

She rested her head against one of the big rocks and let her eyes fall shut.

When she opened them again, the moon was in a different place.

"Oh no!" She jumped to her feet. "I must have fallen asleep!"

"Don't worry, little fairy." Pearl crawled close to her. "Your friends did some work for you."

"What?" Devi stared at the circle of rocks. It was complete, but with much smaller rocks, not the ones she had in mind. "How did this happen?" She frowned as she flew up into the air.

Then she heard a loud snore. She spied Cara fast asleep on the soft grass not far from the circle of rocks.

"Cara?" Devi touched her arm.

Cara snorted.

"Cara!" Devi frowned and gave her shoulder a light push.

Cara snorted, then swatted at Devi. "Go away, I'm sleeping."

"Cara!" Devi shouted and jumped up and down.

"What? What's wrong? What happened?" Cara bolted to her feet. "Oh, Devi." She blinked a few times, then smiled. "What do you think?"

"You must have worked so hard." Devi clasped her hands together. She didn't have it in her heart to be angry at her friend, who had only been trying to help. "That was so kind of you."

"I just wanted to make sure you could go on the trip with us. I came to check on you and you were sound asleep. I didn't want to wake you." Cara looked into her eyes. "I hope you don't mind. I'm sure I didn't do it as well as you would have, but I didn't use any magic at all."

"Cara!" Devi hugged her friend and took a deep breath. "Thank you so much. I do have a bit more work to do, though. You should go home and get some more rest before we leave for the mountain."

"I'll do that." Cara smiled proudly as she fluttered away.

Devi sank down onto the pile of rocks and tried not to cry.

"What's wrong?" Pearl crawled from a rock and onto the back of Devi's hand.

"It's not right." She sniffled. "I will have to redo it or it won't work properly."

"But you just thanked Cara." Pearl lifted her head into the air.

"I did because she did it to help me. Part of being a good friend is being patient with others, even when you don't agree with them or they do something you don't like." She wiped a few tears from her cheek. "Cara did her best because she cares about me. I can't be angry at her for that. But now I'm not sure that I'll be able to go on the trip. I really want to get this project done."

"Devi, it's okay to wait." Pearl crawled up to her shoulder and perched there. "It doesn't have to get done all at once. Sometimes important things take time." She sighed. "It feels like I've been waiting forever to become a butterfly so that I can fly around like the rest of you. Sometimes it's so hard to wait, but I have to be patient. Maybe your project needs to wait until after the trip."

"Maybe." Devi frowned. "I am going to try to get it done, though. If I work very hard—if I take my time and do it right—I might just be able to do it."

"I'll be here to cheer you on." Pearl smiled, then crawled back down to the rocks.

Devi spent most of the morning moving and replacing rocks. When the bell rang for lunch, she realized that she hadn't even had breakfast.

She flew up into the air and plucked a large green leaf from a nearby branch. Then she flew down and placed it in front of Pearl.

"Eat up, Pearl. You have to be strong to become a butterfly."

"Thank you!" Pearl began to munch.

Devi flew to the Mushroom Palace and joined her friends for lunch.

"I can't wait to go!" Fifi fluttered her wings. "It's my favorite thing all year."

"Mine too!" Missy grinned.

"I'm looking forward to it." Cara took a big sip of her nectar. "I'm just so glad we'll be able to be there together."

"Yes, we will." Devi smiled. She finished her food, then flew back to the pile of rocks. It was much smaller than when she'd started, but there was still a lot of work to do.

"Pearl?" She looked through the rocks for her friend. When

she didn't see her, she picked up another rock and put it in place. "Finally." She dusted her hands off and smiled. "Now, I just need one more thing."

She began to walk around in search of the perfect rock. She hummed as she looked. She flew in slow circles as she searched. Hours slipped by. The sun began to set. Devi frowned. Finding the right rock took a lot of patience and she had been patient, but now she wondered if she would find it in time.

"Devi!" Bella flew toward her. "We're all gathering at the bottom of the mountain. It's time to go!"

"It is?" Devi gulped. She remembered what Pearl had said. Important things take time. She would just have to wait until after the trip to finish her project. She was disappointed, but she didn't want to miss the trip.

She was about to fly up into the air, when she spotted the perfect rock.

"I'll meet you there, Bella!" She flew toward the rock.

"Devi, you have to hurry!" Bella put her hands on her hips. "We have to leave right on time."

"I'll be there!" Devi waved to her.

CHAPTER 4

Devi landed on the rock. It was just the right shape and just the right size. She gave it a hard tug. She frowned when it didn't budge. She tugged again. The rock moved just a little bit.

"Let's go, rock!" Devi huffed. "I need to hurry!"

She tugged as hard as she could, then fluttered her wings as fast as she could. The rock tipped forward, then settled right back into the same place. "MOVE!" She shoved it as hard as she could.

Finally, the rock tilted forward and then tipped over. As it crashed to the ground she gasped and bolted out of the way. The tip of her wing caught beneath the heavy rock. She tugged, but it wouldn't come loose.

"Oh no." She sighed. "I guess I have no choice but to wait now."

As she wiggled and tried to get free, she noticed something on a nearby branch.

"A cocoon! Pearl, is that you in there?" She smiled, even though her wing was still trapped.

As the sky grew darker she imagined the other fairies beginning their flight up the mountain. It would take them most of the night. It also meant that no one would be around to help her get her wing out from under the rock. She fluttered one wing.

"Maybe a little bit of magic will do it."

She rubbed her hands together, then fluttered her one wing as fast as she could. She wasn't sure that it would work with only one wing. Since her wing was already so sore from moving all of the rocks, it hurt to flap it so hard.

Her hands got a little warm, but they didn't glow. She closed her eyes and took a deep breath. Maybe if she was patient it would work. She just had to give it extra time, since there was only one wing to flap.

After a few more minutes, her hands became much warmer. They even began to glow. Then Devi's whole body began to glow.

She placed her hands on the large rock and gave it a hard shove.

The rock rolled off of her wing and into the center of the circle, exactly where she wanted to put it.

"That would have been perfect if it wasn't covered in fairy dust!" She huffed as she looked over the circle of rocks with the large tall stone in the center. "Oh, well. I don't have time to wash it off now. I'll have to take care of it when I get back. I'll just have to wait to show my friends what I've created."

She shot up into the air and flew toward the mountain. If she was lucky, they might all still be waiting for her at the bottom.

She landed in the spot they usually left from. There were piles of fairy dust. A few ribbons were stuck in low bushes. A bit of dandelion fluff still drifted through the air. They had already made their wish for a safe trip up the mountain.

She peered toward the distance. She saw no sign of her friends.

"Oh, well." She sighed. "I'll just have to catch up with them!" She flew up into the air.

She'd made the trip enough times to know where to go. Soon the other fairies would stop for a rest near the most beautiful waterfall. She couldn't wait to meet up with them there.

The faster she flew, the more sore her wings became. She wanted to get there as soon as possible, but she soon realized that her wings needed to rest. She landed on a large rock on the side of the mountain.

She would have to be patient.

Usually she was good at being patient. But right then, all she wanted was to be with her friends, celebrating their trip up the mountain.

She sniffled as she folded her wings onto her back. She couldn't use magic to summon her friends, as her wings were too tired to flap.

She hummed to herself as she watched the clouds drift across the stars in the sky. She twiddled her thumbs. Then she tested her wings.

"Ouch!" She sighed and folded them up again.

She wiggled her toes. She counted stars. Then she tested her wings again.

"Oof!" She winced and folded them back up.

"I just have to find a way to distract myself!"

She picked up two sticks from the ground. "Hello there, Mrs. Twig." She looked at the other stick. "Hello there, Mrs. Stick. Are you two doing well?"

"Why, yes!" Mrs. Twig spoke in a squeaky voice.

"No, we're terrible!" Mrs. Stick huffed in a deeper voice. "We're stuck on the side of this mountain!"

"Me too." Devi frowned. "Me too."

She tossed the sticks down and pulled her knees up to her

chest. She closed her eyes and began to think about all the things that her friends were likely doing.

Fifi had probably already tripped over something and discovered an amazing secret. Cara probably had a plan to make sure that every fairy had a chance to swim in the waterfall. Bella had likely invented a way to ride down the waterfall, maybe in the shell of a nut or on a broken branch. Missy would flutter around to help everyone and get herself soaked as she did. Ava would be enjoying every minute and calling out to all the fairies.

"Devi, Devi!"

"No, not Devi." Devi frowned. "Devi isn't there. Devi is stuck on the side of a mountain."

"Devi!"

Her eyes popped open. Was that really Ava's voice?"

CHAPTER 5

Ava swooped down and landed right beside Devi on the rock.

"Phew! I've been looking for you everywhere. I'm so glad that I finally found you." She pulled Devi into a tight hug.

"You were looking for me? But why?" Devi smiled as she hugged the elder fairy back.

"I thought all the fairies were with us when we left the bottom of the mountain. I didn't know that you were left behind." She frowned. "I'm sorry. That never should have happened."

"It's okay. It's my fault. I got so caught up in getting my project done that I didn't leave early enough to meet you. Then I got my wing stuck." She sighed as she looked down at her hands. "I just wanted it to be finished for the trip. I wanted to surprise everyone."

"Oh, Devi, I'm sorry it didn't work out the way that you wanted it to." Ava shook her head. "The other fairies told me how hard you've been working. I flew back to Sunflower Grove to find you, but you weren't there. So I flew up the side of the mountain to look for you. I saw you land on this rock. Are you tired?"

"My wings are very sore." Devi ran her hands along her wings. "I couldn't fly anymore."

"What about now?" Ava smiled. "Do you feel strong enough now?" She placed her hand gently on Devi's shoulder. Her hand began to glow. Devi's shoulder began to glow. Then the glow spread out over her wings.

Devi fluttered them, then smiled. "Yes, they feel much better now. Thank you, Ava."

"Good. Then we'd better get moving if we're going to catch up with the others." She winked at Devi. "Don't worry, you haven't missed too much."

"Yes!" Devi grinned as she launched into the air.

Ava flew right beside her until they reached the waterfall. Just as Devi had imagined, her friends were all using their special talents to make their trip up the mountain even better.

When she landed on the ground not far from the pool of the waterfall, her friends cheered.

"Devi!" Fifi flew over to her. "I'm so happy you're here."

"So am I." Devi laughed. "I'm ready for a slide down the waterfall!"

"Use this branch!" Bella waved it in the air.

Devi grabbed the branch and flew up to the top of the waterfall. As soon as she was settled on the broken branch, she pushed herself away from the edge of the water. The current soon swept her down over the top of the waterfall.

She laughed and shrieked as she crashed down to the bottom. When she swam up out of the water she found her friends clapping for her.

I could have missed all this.

The thought reminded her of just how sad she'd been when her wing was trapped under the rock. Maybe she hadn't finished her project, but she was glad that she'd decided to be patient and wait until she returned to Sunflower Grove to finish it.

"Alright, girls, it's time to move on." Ava clapped her hands. Other elder fairies surrounded her as she floated up into the air. "Remember, this journey isn't just about fun and snacks. We take this journey every year to remind us how important it is to be grateful for what we have. We have our beautiful home, our wonderful friends, and this amazing land to explore."

All the fairies cheered. Devi flew up into the air with them. Yes, she was very happy to be part of the celebration.

At their next stop they were treated to a special nectar.

"This nectar can only be found on this part of the mountain." Ava landed on the wide red petal of one of the flowers. "It's the sweetest nectar I've ever tasted. Enjoy!" She flew into the flower to have a drink.

"I'll bet Pearl would love to taste this." Devi pulled a small bottle from her pouch. She used a tiny spoon to scoop up some of the nectar.

"Who is Pearl?" Fifi landed on the petal beside her.

"A caterpillar I met. She's working real hard right now to become a butterfly and when she comes out of her cocoon after such a long wait, she'll need a special treat." Devi smiled as she dripped a few drops of the nectar into the bottle.

"You're so patient, Devi." Fifi sighed as she watched the drops drip. "I already drank all the nectar from my flower. I wish I would have saved some and put it in a bottle like you. Then I would be able to taste it again before next year!"

"It's good to take your time and make things last." Devi smiled. "But it was still tasty, wasn't it?"

"So tasty!" Fifi flung her arms into the air, then tumbled off the edge of the flower petal. "Oops!"

"Fifi?" Devi flew to the end of the flower petal and peered down at her friend. Fifi had landed in a pile of soft grass beneath the flower.

"I'm okay." Fifi giggled and gave Devi a thumbs up sign. "Just clumsy as usual."

"You shouldn't stand so close to the edge of the flower." Cara flew down and landed beside Fifi. She offered her a hand. "Get on those feet, Fifi, it's almost time to fly again."

Devi put a few more drops of nectar into her bottle, then took a sip for herself. She tucked the bottle into her pouch, then flew up into the air.

"Watch out, girls, I'm getting the first snowball!" Bella zoomed past them and into the air.

Devi laughed as she chased after her.

Soon all her friends were zipping around in a game of tag.

Fifi tried to tag Missy and bumped into Ava instead.

"Sorry, Ava!" she gasped as she blushed.

"It's okay, Fifi. But I need to make one thing clear." Ava snapped her wings loud enough to get every fairy's attention. "No matter what any of you may think, no matter what plans you might have, it's important for all of you to know that I will be getting the first snowball!"

She shot up into the air and flew off as the others chased after her.

CHAPTER 6

Devi followed the other fairies up the mountain. Every time she started to feel a little sad about not getting her project done, she heard their laughter and it made the sadness disappear. The next stop on their journey up the mountain was covered with a layer of snow.

Ava did get the first snowball as she'd promised. "Fifi! This one's for you!" She threw the snowball up into the air, then pointed her finger at it. "Fifi!"

"Oh no!" Fifi gulped and swooped down as fast as she could.

The snowball chased after her and smacked her right in the back of the head.

"So cold!" Fifi gasped and shivered. "So cold!"

"My turn!" Bella yelled as she made a snowball. She threw it up into the air, pointed her finger at it, and shouted. "Cara!"

"Ack!" Cara swooped down and hid behind Devi.

"Hey!" Devi laughed. She ducked just before the snowball could hit her and it hit Cara in the shoulder.

As she gathered snow up in her hands, Devi couldn't wait to

be part of the game. She threw it into the air, pointed at it, and shouted.

"Missy!"

"Devi!" Missy shouted at the exact same time. "Not me, not me!" She turned around and tried to run, forgetting that she was already flying. Her tiny legs pumped through the air, getting her nowhere. Devi's snowball caught Missy right in the back.

"Uh-oh!" Devi gulped and flew as fast as she could toward a tree. She'd almost made it there when Missy's snowball landed right on the top of her head. "Oof!" She cringed as bits of snow trickled down through her hair and along her cheeks. "That was a good one, Missy!"

Soon all the fairies were shivering and laughing.

"Alright, I think we need to take a break and warm up." Ava snapped her fingers and a fire began to burn in the middle of the snow. It was just bright enough to light up the night and strong enough to warm the fairies as they gathered close.

While Ava passed out hot nectar for the fairies to drink, they all began to sing songs around the fire.

Devi sipped her hot nectar and smiled. She was still a little cold, but it was worth it for the fun that she'd had. As she joined in on the singing, something strange began to happen. The once bright and full moon began to fade. Devi stared up at the sky. She loved to count the stars, to learn about them and keep an eye on what they were up to. But it wasn't the stars that were causing the problem.

Thick dark clouds rolled toward the moon.

"Oh no." Devi frowned. "The best part of this trip is gathering together at the top of the mountain for the sunrise. If it's this cloudy, we'll never be able to see it."

"That is too bad." Fifi sighed as she looked up at the clouds.

"Maybe we can do a rain dance and get it over with." Bella jumped to her feet and began to stomp in the snow.

"Careful, Bella!" Ava waved her hands through the air. "Up here that will be a snow dance and we don't want any more of that!"

"You're right!" Bella shivered.

"Maybe it will pass." Devi looked up at the sky again. "If we wait, it might."

"We can't wait long." Cara crossed her arms. "It will be sunrise soon. The sun will not wait to rise. We'll miss it." She shook her head. "There's nothing we can do."

"There must be something!" Missy flew up into the air. "There has to be a way to help."

"Girls, try not to be too disappointed." Ava hovered over them. "Even if we can't see the sunrise, there is always next year. We've still had a great journey, haven't we?"

"We sure have." Devi smiled. "Are we still going to the top of the mountain?"

"Of course." Ava fluttered her wings. "Our journey won't be complete if we don't reach the top. Everyone stay close; it's easy to get lost in the dark. Make sure that you can see one another's glow." She led the way up to the top of the mountain.

As Devi flew behind Cara, she thought about what Cara had said. The sun wouldn't wait to rise. That was true. It always lit up the sky and set again. What Ava said was true too. If they were patient, they would get to see the sunrise again next year. It was still a little disappointing, though.

When a strong breeze blew under her wings, she fluttered them quickly. The weather seemed to be getting worse.

"We may have to turn back!" Ava called out. "Listen close. If it gets too dangerous, I will let you know!"

Devi narrowed her eyes and flew into the wind. She didn't want to have to turn back. She wanted to get to the top of the mountain, even if there was no sunrise to see.

Then she noticed another glow. It wasn't from Cara's wings

or any of the other fairies that flew near her. It was stronger and brighter. She slowed down.

The other fairies flew ahead of her.

She changed direction and flew toward the glow. As she got closer to it, she heard the hum of wings fluttering very fast.

Her eyes widened as she realized that someone was using fairy dust to create magic. But who?

She flew even closer, but the glow around the fairy hid her from view.

"What are you doing?" Devi called out. "We have to catch up with the others!" She looked up toward the top of the mountain, where she guessed the rest of the fairies had gathered.

As she watched, the thick, dark clouds began to pull apart. First, they turned into puffballs, then they shrunk, getting smaller and smaller until they were gone.

"Yes!" a tiny voice squeaked. "It worked! Now we'll be able to see the sunrise."

CHAPTER 7

Devi's eyes widened as she looked back at the fairy. The glow faded away and Missy appeared before her.

"Wow! That wiped me out." She started to drop out of the air.

"Missy!" Devi caught her around the waist. It wasn't easy for her to hold them both up with just her wings, but she did her best. "What did you do?"

"I just got rid of the clouds." Missy shrugged. "I cast a spell —to clear away everything—and it worked."

"Missy, you know we're not supposed to do that without Ava's permission and supervision. Magic can go wrong sometimes; we have to be careful." Devi flew her up toward the top of the mountain.

"I know that, but I just wanted to help. And it worked!" Missy smiled as she pointed up at the sky. The stars were bright, without a single cloud to block them.

"Devi!" Ava's voice rang out. "Missy! Where are you?"

"Oh boy, they're not going to be happy with us." Devi sighed. She pushed her wings as hard as she could, but she could only fly slowly while she carried Missy.

"Don't worry, they'll all be happy when they see that the clouds are gone." Missy smiled at Devi. "I'm so glad you were there to help me. I might not have made it to the top of the mountain without you." She met Devi's eyes. "You're not mad at me, are you?"

"How could I be?" Devi grinned. "We're going to get to see the sunrise!"

"Exactly!" Missy laughed. "What could be wrong about that?"

"Here we are, Ava!" Devi called out when she neared the top of the mountain. "I have Missy with me!"

"Devi!" Ava swooped down. "What's happened? Missy, are you hurt?"

"No, I'm not hurt." Missy sighed as Devi set her down on the ground. "I just wore myself out a little."

"Doing what?" Ava crossed her arms.

"I wanted us to be able to see the sunrise." She looked up at the sky. It began to grow brighter. "It's starting!" She jumped up and down and bolted toward the other fairies.

"Devi, what is she talking about?" Ava stared at her.

"Missy just wanted to help." Devi smiled, then looked toward the sky. "It's happening Ava. We don't want to miss it!"

"Devi, wait!" Ava chased after her, but her voice was drowned out by the cheers of the other fairies.

As the sun began to rise, all the fairies held their hands up in the air. Colorful rays of light shot out of their hands and created an arch that curved over the sun. As the sun rose higher, the arch did too. Ribbons of color spread across the sky.

"What luck!" one of the other elder fairies called out. "It's so nice that the clouds went away. Now our trip home will be so delightful." Suddenly she gasped. "Ava?"

"Yes?" Ava flew over to her.

"Do you remember how to get home?" The elder fairy's eyes widened.

"Of course I do." Ava laughed. "All we have to do is—" She gasped. "Oh no!"

"What's wrong?" Devi looked between them.

"I don't remember." Ava pressed her hands against her cheeks. "I don't remember how to get home. I don't remember where home is."

"That's silly." Devi laughed. "It's just down the mountain and then..." She blinked. Her heart began to race. "And then..."

"And then?" Ava looked into her eyes. "Do you remember?"

"No." Devi stared back at Ava. "How is that possible?" She closed her eyes and tried to picture their home. "I can't remember anything!" She gasped as she looked at the other fairies. "Does anyone remember how to get home? Or where home is?"

All the fairies gathered together, confused and worried.

"I remember!" Fifi flew up into the air. "I remember feeling so happy there. So safe!"

"But do you remember what it looked like?" Bella fluttered over to her. "Is it on this mountain? Is it near the waterfall?"

"I can remember the waterfall!" Cara snapped her fingers.

"I remember it too." Ava frowned. "But that's not our home. We just visited it. Our journey started at the bottom of this mountain. Elder fairies! We must talk!" She gestured for all of the elder fairies to gather close.

Devi looked up at the sky. The sun continued to rise. But the beautiful colors didn't seem as magical anymore. Her chin trembled.

"What if we never find our way home?"

"We will." Cara hugged her. "We will find our way—don't worry, Devi."

"But how?" Bella frowned. "None of us remember where it

is or the way to get there. We don't even remember if it's cold or warm or up high or down low. It could be anywhere!" Bella put her hands on her hips.

"This shouldn't be possible." Devi shook her head. "I can remember so many things, but not where home is. How does that happen?"

"I'll tell you how." Bella raised an eyebrow. "Magic."

"Magic?" Devi gulped. She glanced over at Missy.

Missy shook her head and hid behind Fifi.

"Yes, magic." Bella looked at the other fairies. "How else do you think our memory of home could be erased?"

"But who would want us to forget home?" Cara began to pace back and forth. "No one would be so cruel. Would they?"

"Maybe it was an accident," Missy whispered.

"An accident?" Bella pursed her lips. "How does one use magic by accident?"

"We're all still learning." Devi felt her cheeks grow hot. "Sometimes mistakes happen."

"Which is why we're not allowed to use it for complicated spells without an elder fairy to help us." Cara flew over to Devi and landed right in front of her. "Devi, do you know something about this?"

Devi took a deep breath. All of her friends stared at her, except for Missy, who stared at her own feet. Devi didn't want to get Missy into trouble.

"I just mean—I'm sure no one did this on purpose."

"It doesn't matter if they did it on purpose." Bella snapped her wings. "Our home is lost to us forever!"

CHAPTER 8

"Someone needs to tell the truth." Cara tapped her fingers on her arm and stared at each of the fairies. "Someone used magic when they shouldn't have."

"Girls." Ava landed in the middle of the ring of fairies. "We have a serious problem on our hands."

"We know, Ava." Cara looked over at her. "We're trying to get to the bottom of it. We know that someone must have used magic."

"Did any of you?" Ava stared at each one of them in turn. "It's very important that you tell me. What's been done here can't be undone, unless we know exactly what happened."

"Ask Devi." Cara looked at her friend. "She isn't telling us something."

"Cara!" Devi huffed. She folded her wings around her as Ava looked at her.

"Devi, do you have something to tell us?" Ava held her hand out to her. "It's okay, you can tell me the truth."

"She was working so hard on that project before we left home. Remember? She was moving all of those rocks into a circle." Cara frowned. "She didn't think she would be done on time to make the trip. Did you cast a spell to get done on time, Devi?"

"No, I didn't!" Devi gulped. "I used some fairy dust to move the final rock. But not to get it done, only because it rolled onto my wing. I didn't cast a spell, though." She sighed. "What if—what if someone cast a spell to clear away the clouds? Would that cause something like this?"

"Did you do that?" Ava fluttered closer to her. "Did you cast that spell, Devi?"

"No," Devi whispered. She looked down at her hands and clasped them together.

"Tell me the truth, Devi." Ava placed her hand on Devi's shoulder. "Sometimes you have to be brave, even if you're scared that you will get into trouble. You have to tell the truth."

"Please, Devi!" Fifi's eyes filled with tears. "I want to go home!"

"I didn't do it." Devi frowned. "But I know that a spell was cast to clear the clouds away." She did her best not to look at Missy. "Can you fix it now?"

"Not unless I know exactly what was said during the spell." Ava spoke in a stern voice. "Tell me exactly what was said, Devi."

"I can't." Devi sniffled. "I didn't hear it."

"Devi, I will give you one last chance to tell the truth." Ava crossed her arms. "If you don't tell me, I will be forced to take away your magic. If I can't trust you to do what's best, then you can't use fairy dust."

"Oh, please don't, Ava." Devi blinked back tears. "Don't be upset with me. I'm so sorry."

"Stop!" Missy threw her hands into the air. "Just leave Devi alone! I'm the one that did it. I cast the spell."

"Missy?" Ava spun around to look at her. "Missy, you are the youngest fairy and you know that you are forbidden from casting spells. You haven't learned enough to do them safely yet."

"I know." Missy hung her head. "But I didn't want us to miss out on the sunrise. I thought if I just got rid of the clouds then we would all be able to enjoy it. It's my first trip up the mountain, I didn't want to be disappointed."

"Oh, Missy." Ava looked up at the sky. The sun still climbed. "Sometimes things don't go exactly the way you want them to. That's a time when you have to be patient and wait for the next time."

"I'm so sorry. I was only trying to help." Missy sniffled as she looked around at the other fairies.

"Missy, it's very important that you tell me the spell you cast." Ava flew over to her. "Tell me every word that you said."

"I said, Clear, clear, get rid of the clouds, not a single wisp allowed. Clear, clear, for fairy eyes, so that they can see bright skies."

"That must be it." Ava snapped her wings. "The spell cleared our minds as well—of the memories of our home."

"But why?" Missy shook her head. "That's not what I meant."

"Magic can be very tricky." Ava called the elder fairies over. "It isn't just about what we say, it's about what we are thinking and what we are feeling. If you had thoughts about our home in your mind, then that might be why the magic erased those memories."

"I was thinking I didn't want to go home." Missy gulped. "When you said we might have to turn back because of the weather, I wished that we wouldn't go home."

"Ah." Ava nodded. "Well, Missy, this is a very big problem. By casting that spell, you also cleared our memories of home." Ava sighed as she looked at Missy. "I know you were only trying to help, but now none of us know how to get back."

"It has to be down the mountain, right?" Cara frowned. "Maybe we should just fly down and look around? Maybe we would find it?"

"We might be wandering for days!" Bella moaned.

"Can't you fix it?" Missy looked into Ava's eyes. "I thought you said you could?"

"In order to fix such a big spell, I would need a lot of fairy dust. Even the fairy dust in all of our pouches wouldn't be enough. Since I don't know the way home, I can't get more fairy dust." She shook her head. "I'm afraid we may not be able to find our way anytime soon. We may just have to be patient and hope things change."

CHAPTER 9

Devi could be patient.

She perched on a rock and looked up at the sky. She took a deep breath and let it out slowly. She closed her eyes and counted each beat of her heart. She was very good at being patient. But she was not so good at not worrying.

What if they never did find their way home?

She could remember working on her project. She could remember the feeling of coming home after an adventurous day. But no matter how hard she tried, she couldn't remember where that home was.

When she opened her eyes again, she saw that the sun was nearly all the way up. Maybe if she looked off the side of the mountain in as many directions as she could, she would remember something.

She had started toward the edge when Missy walked up behind her.

"Devi, I'm sorry that I didn't tell the truth right away."

"It's okay, Missy." She hugged her. "I know why you didn't. I'm sorry that things happened this way. I know you didn't mean to cause any trouble."

"I didn't." She wiped at her eyes. "Ava told me not to be upset, but I know all of this is my fault. I know that everyone has lost their home because of me."

"Not because of you, Missy, because of a mistake. If you had known that something like this could happen, you never would have done it." Devi frowned. "Try not to think about it too much. Try to think of other things."

"I don't think I can." Missy sighed. "Except, maybe..." She looked up at Devi again.

"Yes?" Devi looked back at her.

"What were you trying to create before we left? I can remember that. I can remember trying to help and you telling me not to use magic. Maybe if you told me what it was—maybe that would distract me. I'm so curious about it."

"Oh." Devi smiled. "I was trying to make a sundial. Do you know what that is?"

"No." Missy tilted her head to the side. "But it sounds interesting."

"A sundial can tell time by the movement of the sun. Each rock has to be positioned just right. Then you put a large, tall rock in the middle. When the sun hits the different sides of the rock, it casts a shadow that shows what time it is. I thought it would be a fun thing that we could all use."

Missy nodded. "How clever, Devi."

She shrugged. "I wanted to get it done before the trip, because I hoped everyone would see it from the top of the mountain. But I couldn't use music. Fairy dust is shiny and it sparkles very bright in sunlight. If the rocks had fairy dust on them, the sundial would never work." She walked to the edge of the cliff and looked down. "It's funny how I was so worried about getting that project done and now I have no idea where it is. It doesn't seem so important now."

162

"I'm sorry, Devi. You worked so hard on it and now you might never see it again." Missy sniffled. "I ruined everything."

"No, you didn't, Missy." Cara walked up behind her. "Like Devi said, it was just a mistake." She wrapped her arm around Missy's shoulder. "It's always good to want to help, but it's important to follow the rules too."

"I wish I had been patient and just waited until next year to see the sunrise." Missy frowned. "Patient like you were with your project, Devi. You took your time and didn't let any of us use magic, because you knew it was important to do it a certain way."

"You're right, but I wasn't always patient. When I thought I would miss the trip up the mountain, I tried really hard to get the project done, instead of just waiting until after the trip. I got my wing stuck under a rock!" She laughed. "It was pretty funny now that I think about it."

"When we get back home, you'll be able to show all of us." Cara smiled. "I can't wait."

"If we get home." Missy looked over the edge of the cliff. "How long do you think Ava will have us wait here?"

"I'm not sure, but it's a good time to practice your patience." Cara winked at her.

"I sure need a lot of practice." Missy rolled her eyes, then she sat down on the ground.

"Okay everyone, gather close!" Ava snapped her wings. "We need to make a plan."

"I like plans!" Cara flew over, with Devi and Missy right behind her.

"I think our best chance of finding our home is to split up into groups. We can cover more ground that way. If we can just get near it, then I should be able to find the fairy dust and I'll have enough to reverse the spell. But I have to warn you, it may take a long time. We may be away from each other for many days as we search. Each group will have an elder fairy to lead it." She frowned as she looked over the young fairies gathered before her. "I am sorry that you will have to do this, but please remember, as long as we have each other, we always have our home as well."

"That's true." Fifi smiled as she fluttered her wings.

"What if we can't ever find it?" Bella flew up into the air. "Wouldn't it be wise just to make a new home somewhere else?"

"We may have to do that at some point, Bella, but we're not there yet. For now, I would ask that none of you use your fairy dust. We must save it in case there is an emergency." Ava folded her hands in front of her. "I will call out the name of an elder fairy and the names of the fairies that will travel with her. Please listen."

Devi peered over the side of the mountain as she listened to the names being called out.

"Devi."

"Look!" Devi gasped and pointed off the side of the mountain.

CHAPTER 10

"Devi, are you listening?" Ava frowned.

"Ava! Look!" Devi grinned as she looked over her shoulder. "Hurry!"

Ava and the other fairies flew close to the edge of the cliff.

Devi pointed at a shiny sparkling ball of light in the middle of a grove.

"What is it?" Ava stared at it. "It's beautiful."

"Is that what I think it is?" Missy grabbed Devi's arm.

"I think it might be." Devi's heart raced.

"What am I missing?" Ava looked between them both.

"The project I was working on before we left for the trip up the mountain was a sundial. I didn't get it finished in time because I couldn't use fairy dust to move the rocks. It would make them too shiny and they would sparkle in the sunlight. I think that light down there might be the rock I had to use fairy dust on to move off of my wing."

"Ah, so you used magic to get yourself free earlier." Ava stared at her.

"Yes, I did." Devi looked back down at the light. "If it is the rock, that means that it's also our home. Doesn't it?" She looked back at Ava.

"I hope so!" Ava waved to the elder fairies. "Let's go, we shouldn't waste any time. We will only be able to see the shiny rock in the daylight. It will take us quite some time to get down the mountain."

"Can't we just use our fairy dust to transport us there?" Missy flew up into the air. "It would be faster and easier."

"It might be faster and easier, but it's also too risky. We don't know for sure that what we are seeing is the shiny rock. If we use all of our fairy dust and it turns out not to be what we thought, then we will be in trouble." Ava patted the top of Missy's head. "It is a good idea, but it's best if we're patient and save our fairy dust."

Ava led the way down the side of the mountain.

When they stopped to rest in the snow, no one threw snowballs. When they stopped to rest near the waterfall, nobody splashed or played in it.

Devi could tell that all the other fairies were very worried. She wished there was a way to brighten their day, but the day just kept getting darker.

By the time they reached the bottom of the mountain, the sun had begun to set.

Ava flew up into the air. "I'll get higher and see if I can still see the glow." She hovered high above them for a few minutes. Then she swooped back down. "I'm sorry to say, I can't see it anymore." She gathered the fairies close. "Don't be sad, little ones. We will just wait until the sun rises again. Then we will be able to see it."

Devi's heart sank. She had hoped to be home before the sun set. To help herself be patient, she decided to go for a walk. Getting her mind on other things, made waiting seem not so hard.

She sniffed each flower she passed. She waved to the birds that flew above her. She even chased after a squirrel that flicked its tail at her. Soon she was laughing too hard to be sad.

She flopped down on some soft grass and stared up at the stars above her. As she did, a butterfly flew down toward her nose. Devi stayed very still.

She watched as the butterfly drifted closer and closer to the tip of her nose.

Devi held her breath. She stayed very still. She hoped that if she was patient, the butterfly would land on her.

A second later, the butterfly did land right on her nose. She stared into Devi's eyes and slowly flapped her wings.

Devi smiled. "Hi, little butterfly," she whispered.

"Hi, Devi," the butterfly whispered back.

Devi's eyes widened. "Pearl, is that you?"

"It's me!" She flapped her wings and flew up into the air.

"Pearl! Do you know the way home? None of us can remember how to get there." Devi told her about the magical mistake that Missy had made.

"Don't worry, Devi, I can show you!"

Devi called all the fairies to her.

"This is my friend, Pearl. She can lead us home." Devi grinned. "We'll be back before we know it!"

As the butterfly led the way, the other fairies were soon laughing and dancing just as they would have been at sunrise on the top of the mountain.

"There!" Devi pointed to the sundial. "We're home!"

"I'll get the fairy dust!" Ava flew off through the grove. When she returned, she had a big bucket full of fairy dust. "Alright, everyone. Hold your breath!"

She swung the bucket through the air. Fairy dust splashed over everyone. She held up her hands in the air and flapped her wings very fast.

Seconds later, Devi opened her eyes. She saw Sunflower Grove, but she also remembered it.

"It worked, Ava!" She clapped her hands.

"Thanks to you, Devi." Ava hugged her. "You've taught all of us a lot about patience. I'm so glad that we're back home."

"Me too." Devi sighed. She looked at her sundial.

She'd been so determined to finish it, but because she had decided to be patient and wait until after the trip to finish, it was exactly the beacon they needed to get home.

As her friends danced around her, Devi joined in. It didn't matter if it was midnight or sunrise, they were back home and that was plenty of reason to celebrate.

BOOK 5: MISSY

CHAPTER 1

A light mist covered Sunflower Grove as the sun began to rise. Just about all of the fairies were sound asleep. The littlest fairy —the youngest in Sunflower Grove—was wide awake. Missy had been awake since the very first trace of light. She couldn't believe that the other fairies were still sleeping.

Finally, she couldn't wait any longer.

She swooped through Sunflower Grove, ready to wake everyone up.

"Wake up!" Missy fluttered up to Fifi's bright yellow door. "Wake up! It's spic-and-span day!"

"I'm up, I'm up, Missy!" Fifi called from her rose petal bed.

Missy fluttered to Bella's purple door. "Wake up! Wake up! Ava is going to give the chores out!"

"Ugh. Not now, Missy! I can sleep a few more minutes." Bella snuggled deeper under her dandelion fluff.

Missy flew over to Cara's blue door and raised her tiny fist to knock, but the door swung open before she had the chance to.

"I'm up already, Missy." Cara grinned. "I'm as excited as you are."

"I don't think that's possible." Missy giggled as she fluttered toward the ring of towering sunflowers. Ava and the other elder fairies were already gathered there.

Ava held a long list in her hands.

Missy fluttered as high as she could. She tried to peek at the list. As the youngest fairy, every year she always got the easiest of tasks. One year it was collecting fallen petals, another year it was picking up dandelion fluff. But this year, she was sure that she would get one of the big tasks.

She fluttered to the left and then to the right. The letters were far too small for her to read. She swooped down to get a little closer. As she did, a strong breeze carried through the grove, pushing her right into Ava's head.

"Missy!" Ava gasped as she stumbled back. "Were you spying again?"

"Not spying, just peeking!" Missy landed on the ground with a thump.

"Spying and peeking are pretty much the same thing." Ava put her hands on her hips. "Missy, no one gets to know their task before it's given. You know that."

"I know, I'm sorry! I'm just so excited." She fluttered up into the air again. "Can't you just tell me now? Everyone is awake. They're all coming."

"Try to be patient, Missy." Ava smiled.

As the other fairies gathered in the center of the sunflower ring, Ava called out to them.

"Today is our chance to show Sunflower Grove just how much we love our home. We're all going to get chores to do and I hope that we will all enjoy doing them. Remember, when you give your time and your love to Sunflower Grove, Sunflower Grove gives us a wonderful place to live." She lifted the list high into the air. "Are you ready for your tasks?"

The crowd of fairies snapped their wings and cheered.

Missy balled her hands up into fists and flapped her wings so fast that she began to glow.

Ava began to give out the tasks.

"Fifi, you will be gathering acorn pieces to create hats for all the fairies. Remember, we need sturdy round pieces."

One of the other elder fairies held out a large sack to Fifi.

"And watch out for those squirrels." Ava wagged her fingers.

"I will!" Fifi smiled as she took the sack.

"Cara, you will be gathering fairy dust from the cave." Ava nodded. "Please make sure that you have plenty of fireflies with you so that you will be able to see."

One of the other elder fairies held out a pickaxe to Cara.

"Thank you." She took the axe.

Missy sighed. Those were two of her favorite tasks. Her eyes lit up at the sight of the pickaxe, and she loved the idea of chasing off the squirrels.

"Bella, you will be herding the bumblebees today. We need them to move to the other side of Sunflower Grove. The flowers over there aren't getting enough visits from the bees." Ava lowered her list and looked at Bella. "Will you be okay with that?"

"Yes, I suppose." Bella sighed. "I'll need earplugs for all the buzzing, though."

"Here you go." An elder fairy held out a set of earplugs.

"Thanks." Bella smiled.

"Be careful." Ava looked at Bella. "Those bees can get a little cranky."

"I will."

Missy held in a huff. Herding bees had to be the most exciting chore ever.

"And Missy, you're in charge of collecting all of the dandelion fluff." Ava looked up from her list. "As you know, that's a very important job."

"Yes, I know." Missy sniffled. She tried not to cry. Dandelion fluff. Just like last year. It was the easiest job in Sunflower Grove.

While the other fairies flew off to begin their chores, Missy stomped down the path toward the dandelion field. She liked to be helpful. She really did. But she also liked adventure. She liked trying new things. She had hoped that this year, things would be different.

"Oh well, Missy, this is your job and you're going to have to do it." She started to gather the white dandelion puffs that covered the ground. As she rolled them into a ball, she heard the sounds of the other fairies hard at work—fluttering wings, excited shouts, and mysterious thumps.

What were they doing? They had to be having more fun than she was.

She sighed and continued to roll the dandelion fluff. A bit of it broke away and floated up under her nose.

Her nose wiggled. Then it tickled. Then it exploded!

She gasped as the dandelion fluff rolled away from her.

"Wait! Come back!" She chased after it, but the moment she caught it, she sneezed again.

"Oh no!" She groaned as the ball rolled away again. She chased it around the dandelion field until she was so tired that she had to sit down.

As she rested, she heard the sound of squirrels chattering. She wondered how Fifi's chore was going. And then she wondered if maybe Fifi could use some help.

CHAPTER 2

Missy jumped to her feet and flew up into the air. There would be plenty of time to finish gathering the dandelion fluff. A quick peek at Fifi's hard work would brighten her spirits.

She flew toward the woods and landed on a branch that overlooked a pile of acorn pieces. At first, she didn't see Fifi. Then she noticed two large leaves scooting across the soil.

Fifi had chosen a very good disguise to protect herself from the squirrels. But she was moving so slow! It would take her all day to collect the acorn pieces.

Missy knew what she had to do.

She jumped off the branch and flew up into the air.

"I can help, Fifi!" She fluttered high above the ground and watched as Fifi crawled toward the pile of acorn pieces. "Watch out!"

She swooped down toward the pile of acorn pieces and scooped up an armful of them. As she blew past Fifi, the leaves that covered her friend fluttered, then blew up into the air.

"Missy, no!" Fifi gasped.

Squirrels began to chatter all over the woods. They skittered across branches and down trees straight toward Fifi.

"Ah!" Fifi ducked as the bushy-tailed squirrels began to hurl tiny bits of acorn shells at her. "Missy, watch out!" Fifi spread her wings out to shield Missy from the shells. She snatched the young fairy up and flew into the air with her until they were out of reach of the angry squirrels.

"Let me at those squirrels!" Missy squirmed in Fifi's arms and tried to get free.

"Missy, don't." Fifi sighed. "The squirrels are our friends, but they have a natural instinct to protect their food. That's why we have to be sneaky to get the shells. I would have had a whole sack full if you hadn't given me away."

"I'm sorry, Fifi. I just wanted to help." Missy frowned.

"That's why only a fairy who knows how to deal with squirrels is given this chore." Fifi smiled. "Don't worry, Missy. I will find a way to get the acorn pieces."

"I can help with that! I know I can! Wait right here!" Missy broke free of Fifi's grasp and soared through the woods back toward the dandelion field. She scooped up some dandelion fluff, then flew back to the woods. She set the fluff down on the ground.

"What are you doing, Missy?" Fifi watched her curiously.

"You'll see!" Missy grinned. Then she splashed face first into a mud puddle.

She rolled around in the mud until she was covered in it from head to toe. "See, now I look like a squirrel!" She added a bit of fairy dust to smooth out the look. Then she grabbed the dandelion fluff. She shaped it into a tail. Next she used some mud to stick it to her bottom. "Missy the squirrel!" She shook her fluffy tail.

"Oh Missy, I'm not so sure." Fifi covered her mouth as she tried not to giggle. "You look a little bit like a fairy with some dandelion fluff stuck to her bottom."

"The squirrels will believe it! Watch!" She pranced toward the pile of acorn pieces.

Fifi watched, looking like she wasn't sure if she should laugh or shout at Missy.

The squirrels watched Missy from the safety of the trees. None seemed to notice that she wasn't a squirrel. Missy began to collect nice round acorn shells. She tucked them under her arm and tried to get some more. As she bent down to pick some up, a bit of the dandelion fluff wafted under her nose. Her nose wiggled. Then it tickled. Then it exploded!

"Ugh! Watch it!" one of the squirrels shouted. "Now I'm all sticky!"

"Gross!" another squirrel shrieked.

"I'm sorry!" Missy sniffled, then sneezed again. This time her fluffy tail went flying off.

"That's no squirrel!" a squirrel above her on a tree branch called out.

She gulped and tried to fly up into the air, but her wings were too muddy to flap.

The squirrels swarmed around her and scooped her up. They ran off with her, up into the tree.

"Missy!" Fifi cried out. "Missy, don't worry, I'll save you!" She tried to fly up into the tree, but slammed into one of the branches and crashed back down to the ground. "Ouch!" She rubbed the top of her head.

Missy looked at all the squirrels around her. "Please, don't be mad. We were just trying to get some acorn pieces—just the shells. That's all."

"We have to protect our trees." The biggest squirrel huffed. "Just because you're a fairy, that doesn't mean that you can take whatever you want."

"Oh, but we need the acorn shells to make hats to keep our heads safe when we're working in the caves or moving rocks or piling wood. It's very important." Missy looked into the squirrel's eyes. "I'm sorry for the trouble. My friend Fifi was doing just fine, but I wanted to help and I made things pretty messy."

"Little fairy, I have never seen any creature try so hard to help a friend." The squirrel gave her a light pat on the top of the head. "Let's go, everyone, we could learn a thing or two about being helpful from this little fairy. Hop on, little one."

The large squirrel crouched down so that Missy could climb onto his back. Then they raced down to the bottom of the tree.

Missy held on tight to his fur. She had no idea squirrels could run so fast.

"What have you done with Missy?" Fifi waved her fist in the air. "Give her back right now!"

"It's okay, Fifi, I'm right here!" Missy jumped down from the squirrel's back.

"We'd like to help." The big squirrel nodded to the other squirrels. "Get to it!"

Soon all the squirrels were gathering acorn shells and tossing them into Fifi's bag.

"Wow! Missy, thanks a lot." Fifi grinned at her.

"You're welcome." Missy smiled. But she still had dandelion fluff to collect.

CHAPTER 3

Missy flew back to the dandelion field. The large ball of dandelion fluff was there waiting for her. There was still quite a bit tangled in the grass to collect.

As she gathered it up, she felt the softness against her fingertips. It was so soft. So light. So perfect for a fairy that just couldn't handle a real chore. She sighed as she added it to the big ball. She did her best to keep her nose away from it.

She spent a little time gathering more. But her eyes wandered.

She caught sight of a firefly as it darted past her. She watched it fly toward the caves in the mountain. She could hear the faint clink of the pickaxe as Cara dug for fairy dust.

Fairy dust could be created in a few different ways, but it was also found in mountains and rainbows. The caves in Sunflower Grove had lots of fairy dust. But the fairies only ever took just a little—just what they needed—to keep their people nurtured and healthy.

Missy had never been allowed to harvest the fairy dust. She could just imagine how much fun it would be to swing the pickaxe and find a trove of fairy dust.

She decided to take a break from collecting dandelion fluff to check on Cara. She pulled a tiny cup out of her pouch and scooped up some sweet nectar from a flower as she passed it by.

Once inside the cave, the glow of the fireflies showed her the way. Missy held the cup tight in her hands. The dark cave was full of strange sounds and the glow of the fireflies made everything she saw a little eerie.

"C-Cara?" She spotted a long shadow on the wall of the cave.

"Missy?" The long shadow disappeared as Cara flew over to her. "What are you doing in here? It's not safe without an acorn hat."

"I'm sorry, I forgot." Missy frowned. "I just wanted to check on you. I thought that you might be thirsty." She held out the cup of sweet nectar.

"Oh, thank you." Cara wiped her hand across her forehead. "I am very thirsty." She took the sweet nectar from Missy. "Mining for fairy dust is hard work, but it's all worth it when I find some."

"I'll bet there is a way we can find it faster, so you don't have to work so hard." Missy smiled.

"It's alright, I don't mind." Cara sipped the nectar. "This is delicious."

"Why don't you go get some fresh air?" Missy smiled. "I'll keep an eye on the fireflies and make sure they don't get away."

"That would be great—thanks, Missy." Cara ruffled Missy's hair, then headed out of the cave.

Missy put her hands on her hips as she looked at the fireflies. "Alright, little light bulbs, I'm going to put you to work. If I'm ever going to get one of the good chores, I'm going to have to show Ava that I can do things faster and better." She rubbed her hands together. Then she flapped her wings as fast as she could. Her hands began to glow. Then her whole body glowed. She held her hands out toward the fireflies. "Let's dig deep and find some fairy dust to keep."

The fireflies glowed even brighter than ever before and suddenly each one had a tiny little pickaxe. Missy picked up Cara's axe, and each time she struck the rocky wall, the fireflies struck it too. It was hard work—Cara was right—but Missy kept at it.

"Missy!" Cara zipped back into the cave. "What are you doing? Put that down! You can't touch it unless you know how to use it correctly."

"I do!" Missy grinned. "Look!" She pointed to the wall full of cracks.

"Oh no!" Cara gasped. "Missy, this isn't good. Why are the fireflies doing that? Did you use magic in here?"

"Well, I just thought that things could get done faster if there was a bit of magic involved." Missy shrugged.

"Stop!" Cara snapped her wings together sharply.

The fireflies suddenly dropped to the floor of the cave. When they did, their glowing stopped.

In the darkness, Missy couldn't even see Cara.

"C-Cara? What's happened?"

"Fireflies have a very special job. They glow and give us light. They need all of their energy to do that. Giving them another job means that they can't do their first job. Now we won't have any light until they are well rested." Cara sighed. "And all of these cracks in the cave wall will make it harder for me to find where I was working. I had just found a good spot!"

"I'm so sorry, Cara." Missy sighed. "I was only trying to help."

"I know you were, Missy."

"Maybe I still can." Missy snapped her fingers.

She pulled out a bit of dandelion fluff from her pouch. She stretched it out into a nice soft bed. Then she helped the fireflies onto it. She hummed a soft song as she did. Then she took a bit of the nectar from the cup she'd given Cara and spread it over some more dandelion fluff. She took the fluff and began to patch up the cracks in the wall.

"Oh, Missy, that's sweet, but it doesn't work that way." Cara sighed.

As the fireflies began to glow again, their light shimmered on the dandelion fluff. Some of the fluff shined a lot brighter than the rest.

"Why is it doing that?" Missy blinked.

"Missy! You're amazing!" Cara laughed. "Of course! Fairy dust glows around dandelion fluff. Every dandelion has a tiny bit of fairy dust in it. That's why they can grant wishes. I've never thought of using it to find fairy dust in the cave, but just look at it!" Cara picked up her pickaxe and began to dig in the spot where the fluff shined the brightest. Suddenly sparks flew into the air.

"We did it!" Cara cheered. "We found a big trove of fairy dust! Great job, Missy. Thanks for your help!"

"You're welcome." Missy smiled, but she still had a lot of dandelion fluff to collect.

CHAPTER 4

Missy flew back to the dandelion field. She was pretty tired from helping Fifi and Cara with their jobs. She landed near the big ball of dandelion fluff and yawned. Maybe, if she just took a short nap, she would feel like finishing up her chore.

She curled up in some soft grass and closed her eyes. Just as she was about to fall asleep she heard a strange sound.

She tried to ignore it. But it became louder. It was a steady buzz.

She blinked, then opened her eyes. Above her, she saw a cloud of bees. She smiled at the sight of them. Bella flew in swift circles around the bees.

"Hi, Bella!" Missy jumped to her feet and waved.

Bella didn't answer. She just kept flying in circles.

Missy waved and yelled again. Then she remembered that Bella had earplugs in to help drown out the loud buzz of the bees.

She flew up into the air beside Bella and waved until she got her attention.

"Hi, Missy!" Bella shouted. "I can't talk now, I have to keep these bees moving."

"I can help!" Missy smiled.

"What?" Bella stared at her.

"I can help!" Missy shouted.

"Huh?" Bella tipped her head to the side.

Missy pointed at herself, then wiggled her finger in a circle, then pointed to the bees.

"No, Missy! You can't help. You don't know how to do this chore!" Bella waved to her, then flew in a fast circle around the cloud of bees again.

Missy noticed that one little bee had fallen behind the others. The bee seemed more interested in a bright pink flower on the ground than following the herd.

"Bella!" Missy waved at her friend again.

Bella continued to fly in swift circles. If she heard Missy, she didn't answer her.

Missy's heart pounded as she realized that the little bee would be left behind. It might never find its way to the new hive if it didn't stick with its family. She had to help. She swooped down toward the little bee. When the bee saw her coming, it zipped right into the flower.

Missy landed on a petal of the flower. "Little bee." She peered into the flower. "You have to come out now and come with me."

"No!" The little bee buzzed.

"Please, little bee. You have to catch up with your family."

"No, no, no!" The little bee buzzed louder. "They don't let me do anything! They all say I'm too little! I'm thirsty and I want some nectar. But they all say I have to keep flying. I don't want to go with them!"

"Oh dear." Missy frowned. "I know what it's like to be the littlest. I know it's not easy." She sat down on the flower petal. "But if you let your family fly away, you will miss them. Come with me and I will get you back to them."

"No, thank you." The bee's wings fluttered.

"My name is Missy. What's yours?" Missy crept closer to the inside of the flower. She knew that bees didn't often sting fairies, but since this one was mad, she decided to be careful.

"Bizzy." The bee sniffed. "Do you really think I won't be able to find them again?"

"My friend Bella is taking them all the way to the other side of Sunflower Grove. If we don't go now, you might never find them again. Bizzy, I know you're mad, but this is very important." She held her hand out to the bee. "I promise, you won't always be the littlest. You will get bigger and the other bees will need your help."

"I don't think they ever will." Bizzy sighed.

"I didn't think my friends would need my help either. I keep getting these jobs that I don't want. But today I've helped my friends more than they thought I could." She smiled at the bee. "I'll bet you can too if you try."

"I will!" Bizzy flew up into the air so fast that Missy stumbled back when the bee flew past. "I will try! Wait up! Wait, everyone!" She zipped up higher into the air.

Missy flew up after her.

"Oh no!" Bizzy gasped. "They're gone. It's too late!"

Missy looked all around. She didn't see any sign of the bees or Bella.

"Don't worry, Bizzy, I will help you find them." She looked over at the tiny bee and smiled.

But she wasn't sure that she could help Bizzy find them. She didn't know exactly where Bella had taken the bees. Her wings were already very tired from all the hard work she'd done, but Bizzy needed her help and there was nothing more important to Missy than helping others.

She flew up higher in the air and looked over Sunflower Grove. She saw the glow of the fireflies at the mouth of the caves. She saw the squirrels' bushy tails wiggling as they helped Fifi collect acorn pieces. But she didn't see Bella or the other bees.

Missy really wanted to help, but she wasn't sure that she could.

She landed on the flower petal again. Bizzy landed beside her.

"Let's rest for a little bit and then we can look for them again." Missy stretched her tired wings.

"It's too late. It's too late." Bizzy sniffled. "I will never see them again."

Missy wanted to make Bizzy feel better, but she worried that it really was too late.

The flower suddenly rocked as another fairy landed and skidded across the flower petals straight at Missy.

"Hi, hi, hello, Missy!" The fairy giggled as she landed in a pile on the edge of the petal.

"Hi, Ginger." Missy sighed as she looked at the other fairy. "Are you all done with your chore?"

"Nope, not yet." Ginger smiled. "But it looks like maybe you could help me with it."

"I'm sorry, Ginger, but I can't help. I thought I could help. I really did. But I can't. Now Bizzy is lost and it's all my fault." She frowned. "I should have made Bella hear me!"

"Oh my." Ginger looked from the sad fairy to the sadder bee and shook her head. "This won't do, this won't do at all."

CHAPTER 5

"I was only trying to help." Missy sighed as she looked up at Ginger.

"Don't worry, Missy, everything is going to be just fine." Ginger gave her a hug, then blew Bizzy a kiss. "We'll get all of this figured out."

"But how?" Missy looked up at her. "We have no idea where Bella took the bees. How will we ever catch up with them?"

"It's alright, we just have to keep our eyes open and our minds positive." Ginger winked at her. "Let's fly!"

Missy looked up at the wide-open sky. She didn't think that they would ever be able to find the bees and Bella, at least not before the chore day came to an end. Which meant she wouldn't have time to finish collecting her dandelion fluff. But she knew that Bizzy needed her help.

"Let's go, Bizzy!" Missy flew up into the air with Bizzy right behind her. She flew low and slow enough for the little bee to keep up with her.

"Wee! Isn't this fun?" Ginger flew in a loop and then dipped down in front of Missy. "Doesn't this beautiful day just put a bright smile on your face?"

"I'm not so sure." Missy frowned. "I think I would be smiling if I knew where Bella and the bees were."

"We'll find them soon, I'm sure of it." Ginger led the way ahead.

Missy looked down at the dandelion field as they flew over it. She saw just how much dandelion fluff she still had to collect. As much as she wanted to go finish her job, she had a much more important job to do. A lost little bee couldn't make it for long on its own.

A low rumbling sound made Missy flinch. She slowed down and listened to the sound.

"What is that?" she whispered. "Do you hear it, Bizzy?"

"All I hear is my own buzzing." Bizzy shrugged.

"Ginger! Do you hear that?" Missy flew up toward Ginger. Once she was away from Bizzy, she could hear the sound even more clearly. "It sounds like buzzing!"

"See, I told you that we would find them soon! They must be nearby if they are making that much noise, right?" Ginger swooped down and shaded her eyes with one hand. "But where?"

"Something doesn't seem right." Missy swooped down as well. "It's not like any buzzing I've heard before. I think they might be in trouble. We need to find them—and fast."

"You go that way, I'll go this way!" Ginger streaked off to the right.

"Wait!" Missy gasped. "I can't leave Bizzy alone!"

"I'm right behind you." Bizzy flew near Missy. "You're right, I can hear it now, and that sound means that the hive is in trouble."

"Can you tell where they might be?" Missy tipped her head as she listened.

"I don't know. I'm too little to do most things." Bizzy drifted a little lower.

"You're not too little for this. Listen close. You know bees best. Can you tell where the buzzing is coming from?" She hovered right beside Bizzy. She held her breath so she wouldn't make any noise. She flapped her wings slowly, hoping that she wouldn't make a sound.

"Maybe," Bizzy whispered. "Maybe this way?" The tiny bee began to fly toward the ground.

"I'll follow you, Bizzy, but be careful!" Missy flew right behind her.

"Oh no!" Bizzy gasped and nearly dropped out of the air.

Missy caught the bee in her arms. She knew it was dangerous, with Bizzy's stinger ready to sting, but she didn't want Bizzy to get hurt.

"What's wrong?"

"Look!" Bizzy pointed to a large spider web that spread between two towering trees.

Trapped in the web were all the bees and Bella.

"Bella!" Missy shrieked.

"Missy, be careful!" Bella winced. "I can't get free, it's so very sticky."

"Bizzy, stay back!" Missy gulped as the little bee flew out of her arms.

"Everyone is stuck!" Bizzy moaned. "How are they ever going to get free? The spider will come looking for his lunch!"

"But he won't hurt them." Missy smiled. "Right, Bella?"

"He won't hurt me, because the fairies have a pact with the other animals and insects in the woods. But the bees are in terrible danger!" Bella wiggled her whole body. "I just can't get loose! Neither can the bees."

"What are we going to do?" Missy gasped. "Should I fly and get help? Should I bring Ava back?"

"No, there isn't time." Bella sighed. "The spider will find us before Ava could get here."

"Then we have to think fast!" Missy frowned. "Do you have any ideas?"

"I'm sorry, Missy, I already tried all of my ideas. I just don't know what else to do." Bella sniffled.

Missy was surprised to see Bella so upset. She was usually one tough fairy.

"Can't we use fairy dust to get them free?" Missy reached into her pouch.

"No, don't. Fairy dust will only make the web stickier. It's best that you don't use it." Bella wiggled again. "See if you can get any of the bees free."

"Never fear!" Ginger suddenly swooped down toward them. "Ginger is here!"

"Ginger!" Missy put her hands on her hips. "How can we possibly fix this?"

"It's certainly a problem." Ginger stared at Bella. "But it will be just fine, I know it."

"How?" Missy frowned. "How could this be just fine? Bella is stuck, all of the bees are stuck, there's no time to get help and we can't use fairy dust! It couldn't be much worse!"

"Luckily for Bella and the bees, we have two little heroes that are free—and myself, of course!" Ginger smiled.

"We're too little to be heroes!" Bizzy huffed.

"Ginger is right." Missy nodded her head. "We don't have a choice, we have to find a way to be heroes!"

CHAPTER 6

Missy thought about how soft the dandelion fluff was. It was so light and soft, she thought it might just do the job.

She flew back toward the dandelion field with Ginger right on her heels.

"Hurry, we have to scoop up a bunch." Missy began to gather some in her arms.

Ginger did the same.

Missy's heart pounded as she wondered if the spider might have already returned to the web. She led the way back to the spider web and landed on the ground right in front of it.

"What are you doing?" Bella squirmed in the web as she peered at the dandelion fluff.

"It has a bit of fairy dust in it, right?" Missy piled it up at the bottom of the web. "Just enough to help loosen the bees, and then we can wrap them up in the fluff. The dandelion fluff will make the web even more sticky, but its softness will shield the bees from the sticky gunk." She looked up at Bella. "It's worth a try, don't you think?"

"Yes, please!" Bella's eyes widened. "And fast! I think I see the spider coming!"

"Let's hurry." Missy began to wrap the bees in the dandelion fluff. She started with the smallest bee and shortly she reached the largest. With Ginger's help, they were soon all wrapped up in dandelion fluff.

"Now it's your turn, Bella!" Missy flew up to her and began to wrap the fluff around her.

"I never would have thought of this, Missy. It's a good thing you were here to help." Bella smiled.

"Let's see if it works." Missy tucked the last of the dandelion fluff around Bella. "It might make things worse."

"Don't give up hope, Missy. Your great idea is going to save the day!" Ginger gave her a quick hug. "Let's do it together!" She rubbed her hands together and began to flutter her wings.

Missy did the same.

As her hands began to glow, she caught sight of a large spider as it crawled along a tree branch toward the web.

"Oh no, it's too late!" Missy gasped. "There isn't enough time to get them free!"

"What are we going to do?" Bizzy shrieked.

"I know what to do!" Missy flew up into the air, then zipped straight toward the spider.

"Missy, no!" Bella cried out. "Don't get too close!"

"Don't worry, it'll be fine!" Ginger flew after Missy. "Maybe the spider is friendly!"

"I hope so!" Missy gulped as she slowed to a hover right in front of the spider.

"Out of the way, little fairy." The spider lifted one leg into the air and waved it at Missy.

"Please, spider, we're trying to help our friends." Missy landed on the branch right in front of the spider.

"You mean my lunch?" The spider's many eyes stared at her. "Don't worry, I will let the fairy go."

"No, we need the bees. Without them, the flowers will never survive. Don't you like flowers, spider?" Missy smiled.

"No. They're rather stinky." The spider stretched its long legs out and lifted its body into the air. "Be gone, little fairy, you're in my way!"

"I'm not going anywhere." Missy crossed her arms as she stared at the spider. "You can't have these bees."

"You can't tell me what to do!" The spider stomped its eight legs against the branch.

Missy wobbled as the branch trembled. She flew up into the air and hovered in front of the spider.

"Hey there, spider friend!" Ginger landed on the branch in front of the spider. "I'm Ginger!" She waved her hand and smiled. "Isn't it a beautiful day?"

"Little fairies, you are in my way." The spider stomped its feet again. "This is your last warning! Move or I will forget all about the pact I made with Ava. You may be magical creatures, but you're not in charge of me!"

"Be careful, Missy!" Bizzy buzzed as he flew near the web.

"Listen to your friend, fairies," the spider hissed. "Be very careful."

"I'm sure there is a way we can make this all better." Ginger thrust her hand out to the spider. "Let's make a deal!"

"A deal?" The spider stared at her.

"If you promise to leave those bees alone, we promise to make sure that your web is not disturbed as we set them free. I know how hard you've worked on it. It's such a beautiful design." Ginger smiled. "I'm sure you're quite proud of it."

"It is some of my finest work." The spider nodded. "I don't want it torn apart."

"Never fear, we have a brilliant plan that will set our friends free and cause no harm to your web." Ginger bowed to the spider. "Please, allow us a bit of time to do our work and we will leave your web good as new!"

"How?" The spider tipped its head to the side. "It's full of dandelion fluff!"

"You'll see." Ginger grinned. "Just give us some time."

"Fine." The spider huffed. "I will check on my other webs. But when I come back, that web better be in one piece or I will pay a visit to the Mushroom Palace." He waved one foot high in the air. "If you destroy my home, I will destroy yours!"

"Now, now, no need for that." Ginger gave his foot a light pat. "We'll do a great job, you'll see!"

She grabbed Missy's hand and they flew off toward the web.

CHAPTER 7

Missy really did like Ginger. She always had a smile on her face. She always had something nice to say. But right then, Missy wondered if Ginger had lost her mind.

"Why did you say all that to the spider?" Missy gulped as they neared the web. "We can't get the bees free without hurting the web. All of the dandelion fluff is going to still be stuck to it. He's not going to like that one bit."

"I think we'll figure it out." Ginger smiled and shrugged. "Now we have some extra time to think of some new ideas, right?"

"New ideas?" Missy shook her head. "This was my only idea, Ginger. I'm not sure how else we can get the bees free."

"It's a very good idea." Bizzy hovered close to them. "Just do it, Missy."

"But I can't." Missy shivered. "What if the spider really does destroy the Mushroom Palace?"

"Missy, we're going to have to do whatever it takes." Bella huffed as she tried to flutter her wings. "If we can get back fast enough, we can warn Ava and the other fairies. I'm sure they can think of a way to protect the palace."

"I can't do it." Missy shook her head and crossed her arms. "What if they can't think of anything? It's too much of a risk."

"Alright." Ginger placed her hands on Missy's shoulders and looked into her eyes. "If this is the best idea we have, then let's make it work."

"How?" Missy's eyes widened. "Didn't you hear anything I just said?"

"You said the dandelion fluff will be stuck. Why does that have to be a bad thing?" Ginger looked over at the web. "Maybe it can be a good thing."

"That doesn't make any sense." Missy flew up into the air and stared at the bees wrapped in dandelion fluff. "The spider is going to hate it!"

"The spider might hate puffs of dandelion fluff on his web, so we'll just have to turn it into something that he likes." Ginger rubbed her hands together. "First, let's get the bees free. Thanks to your idea with the dandelion fluff, everything is going to be just fine."

"I hope so." Missy frowned. Then she began to flap her wings and rub her hands together.

The faster she rubbed her hands together, the brighter they glowed. She felt warmth spread over her whole body. When she looked over at Ginger, she saw that the other fairy glowed as well. Together, they created a bright warm beam of light that shined right at the large spider web.

As soon as the beam of light hit the dandelion fluff, it lit up with golden sparkles. The bits of fairy dust in it warmed and glowed just like the two fairies did. It was warm enough to melt the sticky web from around the bees' wings and set them free.

"Fly! Fly free!" Bizzy zoomed through the air as the other bees broke loose of the web and the dandelion fluff.

Bella's wings also loosened from the sticky web.

"You did it!" She cheered as she flew through the swarm of bees. "Thank you, Missy! Thank you, Ginger!"

"*We* did it!" Missy grinned. She was so happy to see the bees and Bella free, but when she looked at the web, her heart sank. It was full of dandelion fluff and some holes had been melted in the spider's web. "Oh, that spider is going to be so angry when he comes back." Missy shivered with fear.

"Maybe he'll see the good things about it." Ginger shrugged. "Windows, right? Everyone likes windows."

"Windows?" Missy rolled her eyes. "All he's going to see is the mess his web is in. Ginger, I know you want to see the bright side, but I don't see one here."

"Then we'll just have to make one!" Ginger snapped her wings. "We want the spider to see something beautiful instead of something broken. So how do we make that happen?"

"I can't make spider silk, so there's no way we can fix the web." Missy frowned as she looked over the holes in the web.

"We can't fix it with spider silk, but that doesn't mean there's no other way. Is there something else we could use?" Ginger glanced around. "Bits of leaves? Or blades of grass?"

"No, those won't work." Missy stared at the web. Sunlight danced on the dandelion fluff stuck to it. "But maybe..." Her heart began to beat faster. "Maybe—yes, it just might work!" She grabbed a bit of the fluff and began to weave it through the sticky web. The hole in the web was filled in by the dandelion fluff.

"Missy, that's wonderful." Ginger flew up beside her and began to weave more of the fluff through the holes in the web.

"Stay together! Don't fly off!" Bella huffed as she tried to get the bees to stay in a group.

"The spider!" Bizzy gasped. "He's coming back!" Bizzy flew into the crowd of bees and they all flew off away from the spider as fast as they could.

"No, wait! Come back!" Bella shouted and flew after them.

"What is this?" The spider hissed as it looked at its web.

"Don't you just love it?" Ginger grinned. "Missy was so helpful, she decided to give you a one-of-a-kind web. No other spider in all of Sunflower Grove will have a web like this. You are the only one!"

"A web like this?" The spider plucked at the dandelion fluff. "Who would want a web like this?"

"It's the best I could do." Missy frowned. "I'm sorry, I did try."

"It's absolutely magnificent!" Ginger flew over to the spider.

"Ginger, not so close!" Missy winced.

"Watch this." Ginger pulled back a leaf so that sunlight could filter through the web. When the sunlight hit the bits of fairy dust in the dandelion fluff, the web began to sparkle and glow.

"What's this?" The spider gasped.

CHAPTER 8

"Do you like it?" Missy held her breath as she waited for the spider to answer.

"It's the most beautiful thing I've ever seen!" The spider pointed to its multiple eyes. "And I've seen quite a lot!"

"It is very pretty." Ginger clasped her hands together and smiled as the web sparkled. "And it's all yours. A gift from us— to thank you for your kindness."

"I guess it is true what they say." The spider looked at them both. "Fairies really do make very good friends."

"Yes, we do." Missy smiled with relief.

"Help!" Bella's voice echoed through the woods. "Come back here, bees!"

"Oh, dear. It sounds like Bella needs my help!" Missy swooped down from the tree branch and flew in the direction of Bella's voice. Even though she was very tired, she still wanted to help.

"I'll stay here and finish up the web!" Ginger waved to her as she flew off. "I'm sure everything will turn out great!"

Missy wasn't so sure. She was even less sure when she spotted the bees. They were flying in all different directions.

Bella zipped one way and then zoomed the other as she tried to get them into a group.

"It's no use." Bella sighed. "They're too scared to listen to me!"

"Don't give up, Bella. I'll help you!" Missy thought about what the spider had said. Fairies did make very good friends. But the bees didn't know that. Maybe if they stopped trying to force them to fly a certain way and showed them that they were their friends, the bees would calm down and listen.

"Bizzy!" Missy flew over to the small bee. She whispered her plan into the bee's ear.

"I don't know, Missy." Bizzy flew in circles around her. "I've never done that before!"

"Neither have I, but I think we can do it!" She smiled, as she was sure that was what Ginger would say.

"Okay, I'll try." Bizzy slowed down long enough for Missy to climb onto her back.

"Follow me, bees!" Missy called out to the rest of the bees. She tried not to think about the stingers that could hurt. If the bees saw that she trusted them, then maybe the bees would trust her back.

"Bizzy!" one of the bigger bees shouted. "What are you doing?"

"Follow me!" Bizzy called out. "We need to get to the flowers! My friend knows the way!"

The bees buzzed loudly.

Missy held on tight to Bizzy's furry shoulders as the bee flapped her wings fast enough to support them both.

"This way!" Missy called out, then she pointed ahead of her.

Bella flew beside her as Missy flew toward the flowers on the other side of Sunflower Grove. The bees followed.

Holding on to the little bee wasn't easy. Missy slipped one

way and then the other. She almost fell off of Bizzy's back when they had to dodge a dragonfly. But finally, they made it to the large field of flowers.

The bees gasped and buzzed at the sight.

"How wonderful!" one cried out.

"How delicious!" another cheered.

"Let's go!" Bizzy buzzed.

Missy let go of her as her wings fluttered faster and faster.

Soon the bees were all flying down to the flowers.

"Thank you, Missy!" Bella hugged her. "I wasn't sure I would ever get them here."

"I'm glad I could help!" Missy smiled at Bella. She was tempted to land on one of the bright soft flower petals. She was so very tired. But she knew she still had her chore to do.

Missy flew back to the dandelion field. She hovered over it for a few minutes. There was a lot of dandelion fluff to gather. Her arms ached just thinking about it. After such a busy day of helping everyone with their chores, she didn't have much energy left to do her own task.

She sank down to the ground and sniffled. She knew that it wouldn't be long before Ava began to fly around to look at all of the chores and make sure that they were done. Missy was sure that she would be quite pleased with everyone, but not with her.

After everything Missy had done, her body was worn out and she really just wanted to take a nap. But she couldn't, because if Ava found her sleeping with her chore not done, surely the elder fairy would never trust her with a more important chore.

Missy pushed one foot in front of the other and began to gather the dandelion fluff.

"Ginger would say, sing a song and dance along and everything will be just fine." Missy sighed. She took a deep breath.

She began to sing one of her favorite songs. She pushed the

dandelion fluff along and continued to sing. She took another deep breath and began to sing as loud as she could.

"La la la, going to win this race. La la la, with a smile on my face!" She took another deep breath to sing the chorus again when a puff of dandelion fluff drifted off of the top of the ball and floated right under her nose.

"Ah, ah, ah—" Her nose wiggled, it tickled, and then she sneezed!

The ball of dandelion fluff took off down the path. It rolled so fast that crickets in the grass had to dart out of the way.

"Wait! Come back!" Missy sighed.

She tried to run after the ball of fluff, but she was so tired she couldn't run very fast. She tried to fly after it, but her wings barely lifted her off the ground.

Finally, the ball of fluff came to a stop.

"Thank you!" Missy hurried to get to it, but the moment she did, a bit of fluff tickled her nose again.

"Oh no!" She groaned. "Ah, ah, ah—" Her nose tickled, then wiggled, and then she sneezed!

The ball took off at full speed once again.

"Please come back!" Missy moaned as she stared after the ball of fluff. "This is never going to work. I'm never going to get done in time."

CHAPTER 9

The thought of how disappointed Ava would be brought tears to Missy's eyes. She had tried so hard to do a good job and to help others, but now there was no chance that Ava would think she'd done well. In fact, Ava might even think she'd been too lazy to do her job.

She frowned. "I have to keep trying!" She stomped after the ball of fluff, determined to get it back in her grasp.

She tried to think the way that Ginger did. Everything would go right. But the tickle in her nose made her sure that everything would go wrong.

"Never fear, Ginger is here!" Ginger swooped down from the sky and skidded to a stop right in front of the giant ball of dandelion fluff. "Stop!" she shouted at the fluff.

The fluff just kept right on rolling.

"Ginger, watch out!" Missy tried to catch up to the ball, but she only sneezed again. She sneezed so hard that she flew up into the air. Her wings flapped while her body spun around in a circle.

"Don't worry, it'll be fine!" Ginger called out just before the ball of fluff rolled right into her and then over her. She spit out a few puffs of fluff as she sat up. "That didn't go as planned, which means there must be a better plan!"

"Ginger, I've been trying to get my chore done, I really have, but every time I get near the dandelion fluff, it makes me sneeze!" Missy wiped at her eyes. "I'll never finish in time. I will be the only fairy in all of Sunflower Grove that didn't finish her chore!"

"Now, now, let's not think such terrible things!" Ginger snapped her wings. "If your nose is the problem, then your nose simply can't help!"

"What?" Missy looked at her with wide eyes. "What does that even mean?"

"It means that it's time for you to take a break." Ginger pointed to a patch of moss. "You and your nose stay there and I will take care of this dandelion fluff."

"But Ginger, don't you have a chore to do too?" Missy frowned.

"My chore is already done. I polished each and every stone on the path through Sunflower Grove. I played hopscotch while I did it!" She smiled. "Now, I'm going to help you."

"But if Ava finds out I had to have help, she will think I didn't do a good job!" Missy shook her head.

"Don't be silly!" Bella swooped down from the sky. "I'll help too. We'll have it done in no time!" She began to gather the fluff right away.

"Me too!" Cara flew in from the woods.

"Oh, dandelion fluff, my favorite!" Fifi swooped out from beneath some bushes. She flew straight toward the ball of dandelion fluff. Her feet skidded on the soft grass as she tried to stop. Too late! She landed in the fluff.

"So soft!" Fifi sighed and rolled around in it.

"Alright, we're here to help, not make a mess!" Cara put her hands on her hips. "Let's get to work!"

Missy sat down on the patch of moss and watched as her friends gathered one ball of dandelion fluff each. She wished she could help too, but she knew that if she tried, she would only sneeze. Instead, she could only watch.

"There we go!" Cara grinned as she rolled the dandelion fluff ball to the edge of the field. "It's looking pretty tidy now, isn't it?"

"Yes, it is." Missy smiled.

"I'm done too!" Fifi rolled her ball of fluff over to Cara's.

"Me too!" Bella add another ball of fluff to the group.

"Here I come!" Ginger rolled her ball of fluff over. "Did we miss anything, Missy?"

"I don't think so." Missy blushed. "I'm sorry, I wish I could have done it myself."

"Missy, you're such a helpful fairy." Ginger hugged her. "But it's important to know that it's okay to accept help when you need it too. It's always okay to ask for help."

"She's right." Bella nodded as she patted Missy's head. "You may be very good at many things, but you can't do everything all by yourself."

"You think I'm good at many things?" Missy smiled.

"Sure you are." Cara nodded. "How else could you have helped us all so much today?"

"You did great. I'm just glad I was able to help you too." Fifi placed her hands on her hips and sighed. "All of the chores are finally done."

Just then a strong wind blew through the dandelion field. It picked up the balls of dandelion fluff and tossed them into the air.

"Oh no!" Missy flew up into the air, as did all the other fairies. They chased after the balls that drifted on the wind.

Cara grabbed one of the balls, but her hands tore through the fluff. The fluff flew all over the field.

"No, no, no!" Missy groaned as the other balls tore apart and scattered over the field as well.

Soon the field looked as if not a bit of fluff had been collected.

"What a mess!" Fifi sighed as she flew over the field.

"Don't worry, we can get it cleaned up!" Ginger started to gather the fluff again.

"But not before Ava gets here." Missy sniffled. "It's too late."

"We still have time!" Fifi called over her shoulder as she flew to the other side of the field and right into another fairy. "Oops, sorry, Ava."

Missy gasped as she looked past Fifi at the fairy that hovered there. "Ava?" Her heart dropped as she saw the puzzled look on Ava's face.

Cara and Bella stopped gathering fluff from the field and turned to look at the elder fairy.

CHAPTER 10

"What is going on here?" Ava placed her hands on her hips as she looked between the fairies and the puffs of dandelion fluff scattered all around the field. "Missy, why isn't your chore done?"

"I'm so sorry." Missy folded her wings and frowned. "I just didn't get it done in time."

"But you had all day." Ava looked at Missy with a frown. "You've always gotten it done on time in the past. Did something happen?"

"It's not her fault, Ava." Bella flew down beside Missy and wrapped an arm around her. "Missy was too busy saving me to get her chore done."

"Saving you?" Ava's eyes widened. "What do you mean?"

"Me and all of the bees I herded to the other side of Sunflower Grove. We got stuck in a giant spider web, and if it weren't for Missy, we never would have gotten free." Bella shook her head. "I was out of ideas."

"Ginger helped too!" Missy piped up, then frowned. "But I still should have gotten my chore done. I'm sorry, Ava."

"There's more!" Cara flew down beside Missy and smiled at

her. "Thanks to Missy we now have a new way to find the fairy dust in the caves. It will be so much easier."

"And Missy helped me too." Fifi held out her bag full of acorn pieces. "Thanks to Missy, the squirrels helped me to gather the acorns this year. I got twice as much or maybe even more!" She huffed as she dropped the bag on the ground. "We'll have plenty for this year and next year."

"Wow!" Ava raised an eyebrow. "The squirrels helped you? Even though you were close to their home?"

"Yes, they did. Because Missy made friends with them." She winked at Missy. "I don't know how she did it, but she did."

"It sounds like you were quite busy today, Missy." Ava patted the top of her head. "No wonder you didn't have time to get all this done."

"She did most of it." Bella tipped her head toward the mess of dandelion fluff. "We decided to try to help her, since she helped all of us, but we ran into a wind problem!"

"We're sorry." Cara sighed. "We did our best, but it ended up a mess. We'll get it done, though. Won't we?" She looked at the other fairies.

"Not without a little help." Ava smiled, then gestured to the elder fairies. "Let's go, everyone. Let's all pitch in and get this done before sunset."

As all the fairies began to work together to clean up the dandelion fluff, Ginger started to sing a song. Soon all the fairies were singing along. Even Missy.

Once all the dandelion fluff was gathered, Ava snapped her wings.

"Alright everyone, let's go to the Mushroom Palace to have a feast. After all our hard work today, we've earned it!" She waved to the others as they took off into the air.

Missy didn't take off. She sat down on a rock and stared at her feet.

"Missy, aren't you going to come with us?" Ava crouched down beside her.

"I'm not really hungry." Missy sniffled.

"What's wrong?" Ava looked into Missy's eyes. "Are you sad?"

"I know I should have tried harder to get my chore done. Now you'll never give me a more important job." She wiped at her eyes.

"A more important job?" Ava blinked. "What do you mean?"

"I know that you only gave me this job because I'm too little and too young to do any of the important jobs." Missy sighed. "I wanted to show you that I can do more important jobs, but all I did was show you that I can't do even the easiest job."

"Oh, Missy." Ava wrapped her arm around the little fairy's shoulder. "Is that what you really think? That I asked you to gather the dandelion fluff because it's not important?"

"Yes." Missy looked up at her. "Isn't that true?"

"No, not at all. In fact, gathering the dandelion fluff is one of the most important chores." She shook her head. "I guess I should have made that clear when I asked you to do it."

"How could it be important? It's just fluff!" Missy's nose wiggled as a tiny bit of it wafted past her.

"Didn't you see how important it was today? You used it to help your friends with all of their chores. You even used it to save the bees. Without the dandelion fluff, what would you have done?" Ava smiled.

"I hadn't really thought about that." Missy's eyes widened. "You're right, without it I wouldn't have been able to help as much as I did."

"I gave you that job because I thought you would enjoy it. Not because it wasn't important. I wish you would have told me that you didn't like it." She took Missy's hand and gave it a squeeze. "I want you to do something you enjoy. Next year, you can definitely try something new."

"I think I'm going to have to." Missy giggled as her nose wiggled again. "Dandelion fluff makes me sneeze!"

"Oh dear!" Ava laughed. "No, we can't have that. But no matter what job you have, Missy, never forget that you have a very special gift. You like to help everyone you can. That's something that makes you special, and I'm really proud of the way that you use that gift. Without you, we wouldn't have had such a successful chore day. Now, don't you think it's time to go celebrate?" She fluttered up into the air.

"Yes! Let's go!" Missy flew up into the air as well. She was about to zip off toward the mushroom palace when a bit of dandelion fluff tickled her nose. "Oh no!" she gasped, then sneezed and went flying through the air.

"Don't worry, Missy!" Ava zoomed after her. "I'll catch you!"

BOOK 6: GINGER

CHAPTER 1

Thick clouds stretched across the sky of Sunflower Grove. They looked heavy and dark. Ginger guessed that they were full of rain. She smiled at the thought as she flew as high as she could. Maybe she would get to feel the very first raindrop of the storm.

When she glanced down at the ground far below her, she spotted her friends all gathered together in the center of a ring of sunflowers.

"Good morning!" Ginger swooped down from the sky and landed right in the middle of the circle of young fairies. "Isn't it a beautiful day?"

"Beautiful?" Fifi fluttered her wings as she looked up at the cloudy sky. "I'm not so sure about that."

"Oh, I love how the sky looks before the rain comes." Ginger spun around in a circle and smiled. "Isn't it great?"

"Kind of gloomy if you ask me." Bella put her hands on her hips as she looked up. A big raindrop splashed right onto the tip of her nose. "Hey!" She jumped back as the other fairies laughed.

"It's raining!" Missy jumped up into the air and flew

through some raindrops. A second later she was blown right into Cara by a strong wind.

"Oops! Sorry, Cara!" Missy giggled as she clung to her friend.

"Wow, it is pretty windy." Bella folded her wings tight against her back.

"Everyone inside!" Ava called out from the Mushroom Palace. "Hurry! Quickly!" She waved to the fairies.

The other fairies flew inside, but Ginger twirled in the rain one last time. Raindrops splattered against her and the wind spun her around so fast that she almost fell from the sky, but she still laughed and clapped her hands.

"Wonderful!"

"Ginger!" Ava shouted. "Inside now!" The elder fairy left no room for Ginger to argue.

Her stern voice startled Ginger. Although Ava was the leader of Sunflower Grove, she rarely raised her voice and hardly ever sounded scared.

Ginger flew toward the others as several more raindrops pelted her. The first few had splashed her and it had been rather fun. But these new raindrops—driven by the strong wind—hit her hard on her wings and back.

"We must all get inside." Ava ushered Ginger through the doors of the Mushroom Palace. "I need to make sure that everyone is here. Cara, Missy, will you help me with that, please?"

"Sure!" Missy nodded.

"Already counting!" Cara called out.

Ginger watched with wide eyes. She could tell that the other fairies were feeling frightened. She could understand why. Even Ava was nervous.

Once all the fairies had been counted, they gathered together in the center of the palace.

Outside, the rain fell so hard and loud that the mushrooms around them trembled.

Missy covered her head and sniffled. "Is it over yet?"

"Not yet." Ginger smiled. She knew just what to do. "Listen, everyone, I know that it seems a little scary out there right now, but really storms are a very good thing. They bring much-needed water to the flowers and soil. They wash away any gunk and junk collected in the stream. They freshen up everything around us and they make way for a new bright sunny day."

"That doesn't sound so bad." Missy smiled. As the youngest fairy in Sunflower Grove, Missy tended to be a little more frightened than the others.

"It's not bad at all. It's just part of nature." Ginger shrugged. "And the best part of being stuck inside is that we're all together." She spread her hands out in front of her. "Just think of all the fun we can have!"

"Fun?" Bella squinted at her. "What fun?"

"We can play games and sing songs and tell stories!" Ginger clapped her hands. "It will be wonderful. I know! Why don't we start with hide and seek?"

"Hide and seek is my favorite!" Missy squealed with glee.

"That's because you're so tiny, you can hide anywhere." Fifi pouted. "I'm so clumsy, I always get caught!"

"Don't worry, Fifi. After we play hide and seek, we can play some cards. You love cards, don't you?" Ginger fluttered over to her.

"Yes, and I just learned a new one from Zari!" She grinned. "What are we waiting for? Let's hide!"

Ginger smiled as she watched all the fairies scatter.

"I'll be it!" Cara waved her hand in the air, then covered her eyes.

Ginger flew off and hid behind a thick mushroom stalk. She didn't really care if she won or lost, she just enjoyed the game.

Moments later the Mushroom Palace filled with shrieks and laughter as the fairies darted around finding one another. All the fear about the storm was forgotten.

Once they finished playing hide and seek—which, of course, Missy won—they moved on to playing cards. Hours slipped by without anyone noticing. They shared meals, took naps, and some slept overnight, but most were too excited to sleep.

As day one became day two, all the fairies were singing and dancing. The rain outside provided the beat for them to spin and leap to.

A sudden loud bang made everyone freeze.

"What was that?" Missy shrieked.

"It's okay." Ginger flew over to her. "It was just thunder. It can't do any harm."

"But lightning can." Bella shivered as the Mushroom Palace lit up. "That seemed very close."

"It can't get to us in here." Ginger waved her hand. "But it is very pretty. Maybe now would be a good time for us to tell some stories?"

"Stories sound nice." Missy nodded.

"I have some really great ones about lightning." Ginger smiled as the other fairies gathered close. "You could say, they're electrifying!"

"Boo!" Bella laughed and winked at her. "You really know how to cheer us up, Ginger."

"I try!" Ginger laughed.

CHAPTER 2

Ginger told all her favorite stories. Then the fairies took turns making up stories of their own. But soon they began to yawn. Everyone became quite tired. The storm still rumbled outside. The thunder crashed and the lightning flashed.

Ginger thought about how pretty the world looked in the light created by a lightning bolt. She smiled to herself at the thought of a crash of thunder waking up all of the tiny creatures in the woods and warning them to take cover from the storm. Everything really did serve a purpose. Usually, a wonderful one.

As the other fairies began to lose interest in stories and games, Ginger tried to think of some new ideas to keep them smiling. She even offered to play charades.

"Not now." Cara shook her head as the thunder continued to rumble. "If we're going to be stuck here for a while, I'd better check on the food supplies."

"I'm sure that Ava has plenty stored up for just this kind of situation." Ginger shrugged.

"Maybe. But I'd feel better if I checked." Cara walked off in a hurry.

Ginger sensed that the other fairies were all getting a little restless. She decided she would put on a play to cheer them up. Missy would likely want to help. She looked around for the littlest fairy.

"That wind is really howling!" Missy hovered near a window, her eyes wide as she listened to the sound of the wind.

"It sounds like an angry wolf," Fifi agreed. She clenched her hands together. "I hope it stops soon."

"If you listen to it closely, it's a very pretty sound." Ginger flew up to the window beside Missy. "Just close your eyes and listen only to the sound." She closed her eyes and smiled. "It's almost like a song."

"A song?" Missy shook her head. Then she closed her eyes and listened. Soon she hummed right along. "You're right, it is beautiful."

Ginger opened her eyes and smiled. "See, sometimes even things that seem scary can actually be wonderful."

"Thanks, Ginger!" Missy hugged her. "I'm so glad you're here."

"Thanks, Missy." Ginger smiled as she hugged her back.

After a few more rounds of cards and hide and seek, all the fairies gathered in the center of the Mushroom Palace.

Ava flew to the center of the group and landed on the ground.

"Everyone, I've just had an update on the weather. It doesn't seem like it's going to stop anytime soon. It's still not safe for any of you to go out." She took a deep breath and clasped her hands together. "We're just going to have to stay inside."

"Still?" Bella moaned. "But we've been in here for days!"

"Two days." Ginger smiled. "Only two days. I'm sure we can handle it for a little bit longer."

"But she didn't say a little bit longer." Cara crossed her arms. "She said she didn't know how long."

"You're right. I'm sorry." Ava shook her head. "I can't tell you when, but the storm will eventually pass. Just try to keep your spirits up." Ava flew off.

"Who's up for another round of hide and seek?" Ginger waved her hand in the air and grinned. "I'll be it!"

"No more hide and seek!" Bella snarled. "I've had enough of cards and games and stories! I want to fly!" She rubbed her wings together. "Don't your wings ache?"

"Yes, mine do." Fifi sighed as she stretched her wings. "There isn't enough room to fly in here—not for very long anyway. My wings are getting very sore."

"Soon everyone's wings will be." Cara put her hands on her hips. "Fairies have to fly. If they don't, their wings get very sore and the fairy gets very cranky."

"But we don't have to get cranky." Ginger smiled as she looked at the other fairies. "We can do this. If we stick together, we can get through anything!"

"I don't want to get through it!" Bella's hands balled into fists. "I don't want to stick together! I want to go outside and fly! I want to fly as high as I can go and then swoop down as fast as I can! I want to splash into the stream and then zoom back out again!"

"And you will, Bella." Ginger looked into her eyes. "You just have to be a little patient. Soon enough, we'll all be back outside, zipping and zooming around." She stretched her wings. "Just think of how much fun we'll have then!"

"I don't want to!" Bella shrieked. "I don't want to think about how much fun I will be having. I want to have fun now."

"Bella, when this storm passes, we will all be so relieved. The air will be so fresh and the soil nice and soft from the rain. The sky will be bright and sunny—"

"Enough!" Bella shouted. "Just stop it, Ginger! Just stop talking!"

"Stop talking?" Ginger flew back a few steps as she stared at Bella. "Why? Did I say something wrong?'

"Yes!" Bella flew toward her. "You won't stop yapping about how good things are and how wonderful things will be! It's not wonderful! It's terrible! We're trapped in here with sore, aching wings! We might be stuck in here for weeks! You have no idea! But you keep going on and on about how good everything is! Stop it! No one believes you! No one wants to hear it! Really, I've had enough!" She snapped her wings sharply and pointed her finger right in Ginger's face. "Not another word? Do you understand me? If I hear you say another word about how we should all be happy and cheerful I will lose my mind!"

All of the other fairies got very quiet.

Ginger fluttered her wings as she hovered in front of Bella. She opened her mouth to speak, but before she could, Bella put her finger to her lips to remind her to be quiet.

CHAPTER 3

Ginger was shocked by Bella's words. Tears filled her eyes. She loved her friends very much and she certainly didn't want any of them to be mad at her. It seemed that Bella was quite mad.

"Enough! Okay?" Bella huffed, then flew off to the other side of the palace.

Ginger flew off too, to the furthest, smallest corner she could get to. She squeezed between two small mushrooms and hid in their shadows. Her cheeks burned with heat. She'd never been so embarrassed before.

Did Bella really think she was annoying? She always tried so hard to brighten the days of the fairies around her. She didn't want to make them frustrated or irritated. But somehow, she had.

She wiped at her eyes as a few tears slipped past. She didn't want to think that all of her friends were mad at her, but she couldn't find any other reason for them not to tell Bella that she was wrong. No one had spoken up for her. No one had told Bella to be quiet or at least not to be so mean.

Ginger wrapped her arms around herself and sniffled some more. She wanted to believe that everything would be fine, but right then, it didn't feel as if it would be. She wished the storm had never happened. She wished she had never tried to cheer up her friends. In fact, she wished that she didn't have any friends at all.

She squeezed even further into her small space, and as she did, she noticed a tiny door she'd never seen before—probably because she had never needed to be so small and hidden before.

When she peered through the narrow door, she saw that the clouds had begun to clear. The rain had slowed to a drizzle. The storm outside was over, but inside, she still felt very upset.

She didn't want to face Bella or any of the other fairies, so she flew off through the door. She flew as fast as she could. She flew over the dandelion field and over the stream that ran through Sunflower Grove. She flew past the big mountains and into the woods. She flew until her wings felt as if they might fall off. Only then did she sit down on a thick branch for a rest.

As she looked around the dark woods, she realized that she had no idea where she was. She hadn't paid attention to which direction she was flying. She just wanted to get as far away as possible. Now that she had, it crossed her mind that she might not be able to find her way back.

She shivered and pulled her knees up to her chest. As she rested her chin on her knees, she heard a soft rustle from behind her.

Her heart raced. Was there someone else on the branch with her? A pesky squirrel perhaps?

It didn't sound like a squirrel.

She turned her head and spotted a large hole in the trunk of the tree. She shivered as she saw two eyes stare out at her.

"Who's there?" a faint voice asked.

Ginger nearly fell off of the tree branch. She gripped some leaves tightly and gasped.

"Who are you?"

"Who are *you*?" The voice replied.

Ginger's mind raced. Was this creature there to hurt her? In the past, she would have assumed that whoever it was in the shadows would be a friend. But since she was already upset, she thought that things might only get worse.

"I'm Ginger. A fairy. I mean you no harm." She held up her hands and took a few steps back away from the hole.

"You shouldn't be here." The voice grew stronger. "This is my tree."

"Oh, but isn't there room enough for both of us?" Ginger slowly flapped her wings. They were still quite sore. She couldn't imagine having to fly without resting. "I just need to rest for a little while."

"I'm afraid that you have picked the wrong place to rest," the voice replied. The eyes inside the hole narrowed. "Get away from my tree. Now!"

Ginger gasped. She crept to the very edge of the tree branch, where the branch became so thin that it bowed under her weight.

"Please, what if I just stay here? For a little while? I just need a little rest and then I will be able to fly again." She sighed as she ran a hand along her wing. "I have nowhere else to go."

"Nonsense. Fairies live in packs. I know that you have somewhere to go."

Another rustle came from inside the hole. Then a head poked out. It was covered in long dark feathers.

"This is my home, not a fairy nest."

"Oh! You're an owl!" Ginger smiled as she looked at him. "And such a beautiful one at that. I've never had the chance to make friends with an owl before." She crept across the branch toward him. "What's your name?"

"You're not going to have the chance now either! I don't

make friends and I don't share my tree!" He stomped his sharp-clawed foot against the tree branch.

The branch shook and Ginger almost slipped off.

She wrapped her arms around the branch and swung her feet up onto the top of it. As she pulled herself back up, she frowned.

"That wasn't very nice. I could be hurt. My wings will barely flap—that's how tired I am. What if I fell all the way to the ground?" She crossed her arms.

"It seems to me that if a fairy can't fly, she shouldn't land in a tree." The owl ruffled his feathers. "If you fall, if you fly—it makes no difference to me. You're the one that chose to fly as far as you did."

"You're right, that was my choice." Her eyes filled with tears again as she thought of the fairies in Sunflower Grove. "You're not the only one that doesn't want to be friends with me."

"I don't want to be friends with anyone." The owl fluffed his wings. "In fact, I've never had a friend."

"Never?" She stared at him. "Not one?"

CHAPTER 4

"Nope, not a single friend." The owl stared back at Ginger. "It's been wonderful to be alone all this time. I was doing just fine, in fact, until you landed here. So, you can see why I'm bothered. Now scat!" He stomped his foot against the branch again.

This time Ginger lurched forward and fell into the owl's soft feathers.

"Watch it!" He scowled as he pushed her back up to her feet. "You really are a terrible being, aren't you?"

"Am I?" She sniffled. "Maybe. Maybe I am." She sat back down on the branch and tried not to cry.

"That's not leaving, that's sitting." The owl fluttered his feathers, then marched over to her. "Go on, I'm sure there is another tree that you could rest on."

"I can't fly to it—not until I rest." She crossed her arms. "Just go back in your hole. You won't even know that I'm here. I'll be very quiet." She did her best to hold back her tears.

"Oh, there's nothing worse than a sad fairy." He huffed. "You're not going to drip fairy dust all over my tree, are you? This is a non-magic zone. I've seen fairies like you zipping around here and glowing. I've seen it all from my home. Until now, they always stayed away." He glared at her. "What's it going to take for me to get rid of you?"

"Why are you so mean?" Ginger crossed her arms. "Why is everyone so mean?"

"You don't think it was mean to land in front of my home and disturb me?" The owl flapped his wings. "I didn't invite you here. I didn't stick my head outside today and say, oh, I'd love for a fairy to come interrupt my peace and quiet. Did I? So, who is the mean one here?" He began to march back and forth across the branch. "You don't own the woods just because you're magical. We plain old non-magical creatures have a right to our homes and our peace."

"I'm sorry." Ginger sighed and wiped at her eyes. "I guess I should have thought about that before I landed. I keep doing everything wrong." She frowned as her heart sank.

Maybe Bella was right when she'd said what she did. Maybe Ginger really was just a pest that no one wanted around. Clearly, the owl didn't want her there.

"I'll go, as soon as I can, I promise." She looked up through the leaves that hung off the next heavy branch above her. The last bit of sunlight streamed through them. "It's beautiful." She sighed as she admired the way the sun painted the leaves.

"What is?" The owl tilted his head to look.

"The sun, the leaves." She smiled. Her heart felt a little lighter.

"No, it's not beautiful. The sun is there to burn you up. The leaves will fall and make quite a mess. What is beautiful about any of it?" He used his beak to free a bit of leaf from his feathers. "See? Already they're starting to make a mess."

"Maybe you're right." She frowned. "What does it matter if it's beautiful anyway? I'm still all alone."

"Alone can be a good thing." He puffed out his chest. "I like it just fine."

"What do you know?" She sighed. "You've never been off of this branch. How do you even survive?"

"Maybe I feast on little fairies that land in front of my house!" He stomped his talons on the branch so hard that it shook.

"Oh no!" Ginger gulped and clung to the branch again. "You wouldn't! You couldn't! The fairies have a pact with the creatures!"

"Pact, shmact! That has nothing to do with me!" He spread his wings wide and narrowed his fierce eyes. "I live by my own rules!"

"No, don't!" Ginger shrieked. "I'll go, I promise. I'll go right now!"

"Good." The owl folded his wings, then chuckled. "You looked so scared. As if I would ever take a bite of a fairy. I would get wing stuck in my teeth!"

"You're the meanest creature I've ever met!" Ginger glared at him. "I think everyone should have a friend. Everyone should have a good life. But you? I'm not so sure that you deserve any of that."

"That's fine with me, I don't want it! Didn't you say you were going to leave?" He waddled back to the hole in the tree. "Don't make me come back out here. I've already wasted enough of my time."

"I'm sorry if I interrupted your brooding and glaring." Ginger pushed herself to her feet, then she tried to flap her wings. They trembled with pain. But she knew that she had to fly. If she didn't, who knew what the owl might do? It wasn't safe for her to fly, but she had no choice. It was just another bad thing about her already very bad day.

Maybe the owl had a point. Maybe things weren't ever good. Maybe she'd just fooled herself into believing that they were.

She walked to the edge of the branch and peered down at

the ground. It was a very long way to go. She hoped that if she flew just a little, she would be able to land on another branch. But what were the chances of that? She guessed that her already bad day would only get worse.

She jumped into the air and began to flap her wings. At first she hovered. She smiled with relief. Maybe her wings would carry her after all. But a second later, she began to drop from the sky.

"Oh no!" She gasped as she fell faster toward the ground. Her wings fluttered, but only from the wind. She couldn't get them to flap.

CHAPTER 5

The ground raced toward her. She gulped and reached for anything that she could grab. Her hands found a thin twig that grew from a thick branch. She clung tightly to it. It wasn't strong enough to hold her for long, but at least it had stopped her from falling. But for how long?

She tried to squirm back up the twig to reach the thick branch, but she wasn't strong enough to pull her body up.

"Help!" she cried out. A second later she wondered why.

No one would help her. No one cared. She was all alone. She sniffled as tears streamed down her cheeks.

No, there was no bright side to find. Things were not going to get better.

"Hold on, little fairy!" The owl swooped down through the air. "I'll save you!"

Ginger clung to the tiny twig. Her feet swung through the air. She wished she hadn't flown so high. She wished she hadn't flown so far that her wings couldn't flap. But most of all she wished she'd never met that pesky owl.

"You stay away from me!" she shouted at the owl as he hovered near her. "You are the meanest creature I've ever met."

"Really?" His eyes widened. "I'm sure you haven't met all the other creatures around here. I can't be certain, but I don't think I would be the meanest." He held out one wing to her. "Climb on. I'll get you back onto the branch."

"Or you'll fling me to the ground!" Ginger shook her head and held tighter to the twig. "No, just stay away from me!"

"You'd rather fall to your doom than give me a chance?" The owl flapped his long wings. "That doesn't seem very wise to me."

"You made me fly off the branch in the first place! You wanted me to fall!" She gasped as the twig began to break away from the branch.

"I didn't know you really couldn't fly. I thought you were lying. I don't want you near my home, but I don't want you to splat against the ground either. Let's go." He held his wing out. "I may not be the nicest creature, but I'm all you have right now."

Ginger sighed as she realized the owl was right. Still, as she climbed onto his wing, she was frightened. How could she trust him after he'd been so mean to her?

He flew up to the branch beside his home and landed on it. He held out his wing so that she could climb down.

"There now." He nodded to her. "Safe and sound."

"Why did you help me?" She stared at him. "I thought you hated me!"

"Just because I don't want company doesn't mean I hate you." He folded his wings around his body. "I just prefer to be alone. But you can rest for a little while—until you're ready to fly. Just don't plan on sticking around."

"But why?" She sat down on the branch. "What's so bad about me being around?"

"I'm sorry." The owl looked down at the long claws on his feet. "I don't like to leave my home. It's safe there. Nothing can hurt me if I just stay put. I don't like to meet new creatures because they probably won't like me. When I'm alone, I'm safe." He shrugged. "It's just the way I've always been."

"That sounds very lonely." Ginger frowned. "But it also sounds pretty good. I thought I had a lot of friends, but it turns out they don't like me at all." She shook her head. "Maybe you're right. Maybe it is better to be alone."

"I've never had any complaints." The owl smiled. "Me, myself, and I have the best talks."

"You're funny." Ginger laughed.

"Do you think so?" His eyes widened. "No one has ever told me I was funny before."

"How could they? You don't ever meet anyone." She crept a little closer to him. "Maybe I was wrong. Maybe you're not mean at all."

"Back away!" He flapped his wings and stumbled back against the tree trunk. "Don't get too close. Remember, I don't want any friends!"

"It's too late for that!" She grinned as she flung herself toward him with her arms spread wide. She landed in his soft feathers and hugged him. "I'm already your friend."

"Oh no," he moaned. "This is awful. This is just terrible."

"Yes, it is." She giggled and hugged him tighter. "It's you and me, buddy. Wait, I don't even know your name." She looked up at him. "What is it?"

"I'm not telling you." He huffed.

"Okay, then I'll just hug it out of you!" She squeezed tighter.

"No, no! That's enough! If I tell you, you have to promise never to hug me again. Okay?" He looked into her eyes.

"Okay." She let go of him and sat back down on the branch.

"I'm Hal." He stared at her. "And you're not my friend."

"Maybe I'm not yet. But you're my friend. You saved me." She smiled. "That means you will always be my friend."

"See, this is why I don't leave my home!" He marched back into the hole in the tree. "You stay out there, I'll stay in here and as soon as you're strong enough, you'd better fly away!"

"Whatever you say, Hal." She wiggled her fingers at him, then she curled up on the branch.

She did want to rest her wings. She closed her eyes and soon fell right to sleep. She hoped she would have good dreams. But instead, her dreams were filled with the memory of Bella shouting at her.

She woke up just as grumpy as she'd felt when she went to sleep. Only now, huge eyes peered down at her.

"Ah!" she gasped.

CHAPTER 6

"It's about time you woke up." Hal took a few steps back. "The moon is high in the sky. How long did you plan to sleep?"

"The moon?" Ginger blinked as she looked up at the owl. "But that means it's the middle of the night!"

"Exactly." He sat back and preened his feathers. "I've never seen someone sleep right through to the middle of the night."

"Oh." She laughed as she sat up. "That's right. You're nocturnal. You're awake all night."

"Yes. And?" He looked at her.

"And I'm not. I'm usually awake during the day and sleep all night." She stretched her arms above her head. "But I think I've slept enough."

"Odd that you would want to be awake during the day. It's always so noisy and bright." He squinted at her. "Are you strong enough to fly now?"

"I think I am." She flapped her wings slowly. "My wings feel stronger."

"Good." He gestured to the night sky. "Get moving!"

"I'd hate to leave without repaying you for saving me."

Ginger crept close to him. "Isn't there some way that I can help you?"

"Yes, you can help me by leaving. I thought I made that clear?" He blinked.

"Hal, you could have let me fall. You would have been all alone again. If you really didn't care about anyone else, you wouldn't have saved me." She crossed her arms. "I don't think you're mean at all. I think you're just scared."

"Of course I am. Everything is dangerous." He tightened his wings around him. "But as long as I'm in my home, I'm safe."

"But you're also alone." She frowned. "I used to think that everything would always be just fine. I would always look at the bright side of things. Now I'm not so sure about that. But I do know that there is a lot to see and experience and enjoy. Maybe I can help you to see some beautiful things so that you won't be afraid to come out of your home?"

"Or maybe you can leave me alone!" He huffed and stomped back into the hole in the tree. "Fly off! Go home! Just go!"

Ginger didn't want to leave. Mostly because she knew that once she did, Hal would be alone again. Maybe she wasn't sure if things would ever be okay again, but she did know that it was hard to be alone. She missed her friends so much, even if they didn't feel the same way about her. But she didn't want to make Hal any angrier than she already had.

She jumped into the air and started to fly off through the woods. In the moonlight everything looked eerie. She wasn't sure which way to go. She'd flown so far that she didn't know how to get back. Not that it mattered, since she doubted anyone would want to see her. That gave her an idea.

She flew back to Hal's tree and landed with a thump just outside of his hole.

"Hal!"

"Oh no!" He flapped his wings and muttered. "Are you back?"

"Yes, I am." She sniffled. "I can't find my way home. I'm not used to flying at night. I need some help."

"Help? Haven't I already helped you enough?" He crept out onto the branch. "I'm sure someone else out there can help you."

"But you're the only one I trust. There are all kinds of predators in the woods at night, Hal. I'll only be safe if you come with me." She sighed. "You don't want me to end up a splat on the ground, remember?"

"I remember." He hooted. "Fine. I will take you to the edge of the woods. But that is as far as I will go. I like to stay in my home. I only go out now and then to hunt. But I know where the edge of the woods is. I'll show you there and that's it. Got it?"

"Got it." She smiled as she launched into the air. "I'll bet I can fly faster than you!"

"I doubt that, fairy!" He hooted as he flew up into the air.

Ginger darted off ahead of him, but seconds later he caught up and flew right past her.

"I thought you didn't know the way?"

"I don't." She flew beside him. "But I still wanted to race."

"Racing can be dangerous. You should be more careful."

"You're right, I'm sorry." She flew a bit lower, right over a small waterfall. "Look at that, Hal. Isn't it beautiful?"

"A waterfall?" He followed her down closer to the waterfall. "It's not beautiful at all. It's dangerous. If you get caught up in its current, it will sweep you right over and you'll be dashed on the rocks." He pointed to the large rocks in the pond below the waterfall.

"That may be true, but it's still a lot of fun to splash in!" She swooped down through the air and skimmed the tips of her toes in the rushing water.

"Ginger! Stop!" Hal swooped down as well and grabbed her with his talons. He pulled her up out of the water. "That is not safe at all!"

"But the water feels so good." Ginger squirmed out of his grasp. "Just dip your feathers in, you'll see. It's okay. As long as you don't go all the way in, you'll be just fine."

"I don't think it's a good idea." He shook his head.

"You're going to love it!" She grabbed his wing. "Let's go, we'll do it together."

"Ginger, it's better to just avoid anything risky. Okay?" Hal tried to wiggle his wing free. "I just want to go back home!"

"Just one little splash!" She smiled, then dipped her hand down into the rushing water. She scooped some up and tossed it at Hal.

"You horrible winged beast!" Hal shrieked as the cold water struck his feathers.

CHAPTER 7

Ginger dodged the swift swat of the owl's wing, but just barely. She gulped as the fierce creature scowled at her.

"I never should have helped you! I should have stayed in my home where it's safe—and dry!" He shook the drops of water from his wing. Then he blinked. He looked down at his feathers. Then he shook them again. He looked up at Ginger.

"Wait, don't attack!" She held up her hands. "I only did it because I thought you would like it!"

"You thought I would like it?" He stared at his damp wing.

"Yes. I did. I'm sorry." She fluttered away to a safe distance.

"I did!" He looked back up at her. "I did like it! That water feels wonderful on my feathers!"

"But you were so angry." She inched back toward him. "Is this some kind of trick?"

"When I shook the water off, it felt so lovely!" He smiled. "Refreshing! I have to feel it again!" He flew closer to the waterfall.

"Just put the edge of your wing in." Ginger warned as she flew beside him. "If you put it too far into the water, the current will catch you."

"This is great!" Hal splashed his wing into the water. "Look what I can do!" He swung his wing through the water and sent a shower of water straight at Ginger.

"Hey!" She laughed and gulped and coughed as the water splashed her entire body. She fluttered her wings quickly to get the water off. "Hal, that isn't fair! I barely splashed you!" She wiped water from her eyes, only to find the air beside her empty. "Hal?" She blinked. "Where did you go?"

"I don't like this! I don't like this at all!" Hal gasped as he started to drift over the edge of the waterfall.

"Oh no! Never fear, Hal, I'll save you!" Her heart filled with joy as she rushed toward him. Of course she would save him! Of course everything would be just fine!

She reached into the water, grabbed his wet feathers, and tugged. Then she and Hal flew right over the side of the waterfall and down into the rocky pond below.

"Ow!" Hal groaned as he landed on a rock. "That is not how you save someone, fairy."

Ginger untangled herself from Hal's feathers and gulped down air. She had swallowed far more water than she should have.

"I'm sorry." She coughed. "I thought I would be able to lift you. I thought everything would be fine."

"I'm an owl. You're a fairy." He winced as he tried to move. "How did you think that would work?"

"I don't know." She sighed as she looked him over. "Are you okay?"

"Am I okay?" He stared at her. "What do you think? I just got swept over a waterfall and dashed into some rocks. No, I'm not okay." He tried to fly up into the air, then shrieked. "Oh no, I think my wing is broken." He drifted back down to the top of the rock.

"Are you sure?" Ginger reached out to touch his wing.

"Don't touch it!" He jerked it away, then shrieked again. "Oh, ow, ow, ow, yes, it's broken!" he whimpered. Then he glared at Ginger. "This is all your fault!"

"What do you mean?" Ginger frowned. "I didn't make you fall into the water."

"But if you had never come here, I never would have left my home and I wouldn't have a broken wing right now." He flapped his other wing. "I knew I never should have talked to you. Only bad things happen to me."

"That's not true. It can't be." Ginger smoothed down the feathers on the top of his head.

"It is true. Nothing good has ever happened to me. That's why I stay in my home. It's the safest place to be." He sighed as he looked at his hurt wing. "This is what happens when I don't."

"Sometimes we do get hurt. There's no way to always be safe." She frowned. "But usually the good things outweigh the bad."

"Like what? What's good about any of this?" He tried to lift his wing and gulped. "Oh, it hurts so much!"

"I know it does. I can fix it." She reached into her pouch to pull out some fairy dust. But the dust wasn't dust. It was mush from getting wet in the waterfall. "Oh dear, this won't work. Do you think you can fly at all?" She frowned.

"I can try." He jumped into the air and tried to flap his wings. "Oh no! Nope! That's all bad!" He landed back on the rock. "I can't fly. I'm sorry, but it hurts too much." He looked up at the bright moon above him. "I guess this is where it all ends. I never should have left my home."

"This isn't where it ends! If you can't fly, then I'll fly." Ginger looked into his eyes. "I'll go and get help and bring help back to you."

"From who?" Hal ruffled his feathers. "Those fairies that

were so mean to you? They're not going to want to help you or me."

"They will." Ginger took a deep breath. "I know they will."

"Sure, sure." He shook his head. "Go on, I know you're not going to come back."

"Of course I will." Ginger jumped up into the air and fluttered her wings. "Hal, I'll come back and I'll bring help."

"Sure, sure." He waved his good wing at her. "Go on. Just get out of here." He hung his head as the moon shined down on him.

Ginger frowned. She'd tried to make a new friend. Hal was right. He had gotten hurt because of her. If he had stayed in his tree, he never would have broken his wing.

CHAPTER 8

Ginger flew off in the direction that she guessed would lead her to Sunflower Grove. She couldn't be certain, as everything looked so different at night.

"Maybe I'll never get there. Maybe I'll just fly in circles." She frowned as her thoughts grew heavier and heavier. Of course, many things could go wrong, and so far, it seemed that everything that could go wrong had gone wrong. But Hal needed her help and if she didn't try her hardest to get it for him, then he was right—she wasn't ever his friend. Not that he would want to be friends with her after his wing had gotten broken.

She flew faster. She flew so fast that she didn't notice a dark patch hanging from the branch of a tree until she flew right into it.

"Ow! What was that?" Ginger twisted and tumbled as she fell toward the ground.

"Who was that is more like it!" a squeaky voice cried out.

Ginger landed on the back of a bat who had swooped down to catch her.

"Don't you know it's not polite to fly into creatures?" the bat squeaked as she twisted her head to look up at Ginger.

"I didn't mean to." Ginger sighed. "I just can't do anything right these days."

"Oh, now, now, that's no way to think." The bat flew up into the air to the branch where she'd been hanging. "Where are you going in such a hurry?"

"To Sunflower Grove. At least, I think I am. But I'm not sure of the way." Ginger patted the top of the bat's head. "Thank you for saving me. I didn't hurt you when I flew into you, did I?"

"No, I'm fine." The bat fluttered her wings. "See? But you sure weren't going toward Sunflower Grove. Are you lost?"

"Very." Ginger sniffled.

"I'm Betsy." The bat fluttered her wings again. "What's your name?"

"Ginger. But you don't want to be friends with me, Betsy. I either make my friends mad or hurt them." She crossed her arms.

"Now that's just silly." Betsy laughed. "I'm sure you're a great friend. Why do you think such sad things?"

"I used to be very cheerful." Ginger smiled a little. "But I guess I was too cheerful. My friends didn't like it. Now I see why. There really isn't anything to be cheerful about. Everything always goes wrong."

"One thing went right. You met me." Betsy flapped her wings. "I'll get you back to Sunflower Grove. If your friends really don't like you because you are cheerful, then that is sad. But are you sure that's the case? Sometimes sadness plays a trick on us."

"What kind of trick?" Ginger looked up at the bat.

"Sometimes, when we feel a little bit sad, it makes us see everything that happens as sad. Then we get sadder—and even sadder yet." She shook her head. "It's no fun. But luckily, all we have to do is cheer up and then everything won't seem so bad."

"Now you sound like me—or like I used to sound." Ginger smiled. "Thanks for showing me the way to Sunflower Grove."

"Let's go! It's getting close to morning and I'd rather be asleep than flying when the sun comes up." She grinned. "Follow me!"

Betsy flew through the air.

Ginger followed just behind her. Maybe Betsy was right. Maybe Ginger was wrong about her friends not wanting to be friends with her anymore. She had flown off before they had a chance to talk about anything.

"Here we are." Betsy landed on a tree branch just outside of Sunflower Grove. "I'm sure you know the way from here."

"I do! Thank you, Betsy!" Ginger flew toward Sunflower Grove with her heart beating fast.

Would the others know that she'd left? Would they be happy to see her? She doubted it. But she still hoped they might greet her with open arms.

When she landed near the Mushroom Palace, she noticed that everything was dark and still. She looked up at the sky. The moon had moved, but it was still quite high. She guessed that everyone was sleeping.

She didn't want to wake Ava if she didn't have to. Instead, she flew to Cara's home.

"Cara?" she called through the window. "Cara, can you help me, please?"

There was no answer. Maybe Cara was mad at her after all.

She flew to Fifi's window. "Fifi, are you awake? Can you help me, please?" She hovered near Fifi's window. There wasn't a movement or a sound.

So Fifi was angry too.

She flew to Missy's home. Missy always wanted to help.

Even if Missy was mad at her, Ginger was sure that the young fairy would still help.

She hovered outside of Missy's window.

"Missy!" she called out louder than she had before. "Missy, I need your help!"

Missy's room stayed dark and quiet.

Ginger took a few steps back, stunned. Were all of her friends ignoring her?

"Hello?" she called out. "Hello? Will anyone help me? Please!" She waited in the center of Sunflower Grove. Surely someone would come to help her.

After several minutes, she realized that no one was coming. Her stomach twisted into knots.

"Fine! I don't need your help anyway!" She flew back off into the woods.

As she made her way back to the waterfall, the sun began to rise. She saw the splash of colors across the sky. But she didn't find it beautiful. It was just another day. Another day that she would have to spend alone.

"Hal?" She called out for the owl. She didn't know just how to get back to him.

"Who? Who wants to know?" Hal shouted back from a branch above her.

CHAPTER 9

"Hal!" She gasped as she looked up at him. "How did you get up there?"

"Turns out my wing wasn't broken." He waved it in the air. "It just needed a bit of a rest. I came looking for you to tell you not to worry, but I guess you found me instead."

"You flew all this way, all on your own?" Ginger stared up at him. "That was quite brave of you."

"It wasn't as bad as I thought it would be." He flapped his wings, then flew down to the ground.

"I hope you're not still angry at me." She frowned.

"I'm not. I had a lot of fun. I'm the one who dipped my wing in too far; you tried to warn me." He walked around her. "What's with the sad face? You couldn't find your home?"

"Oh, I found it alright." She crossed her arms. "But my friends didn't want anything to do with me. None of them would help me."

"If that's how they're acting, then they weren't very good friends to start with, were they?" He smiled as he looked at her. "I know what a friend is now. I really didn't think you'd come back to help me. But you did. That shows me you really are my friend. Don't worry about those mean fairies. It's you and me, right?"

"You're right." Ginger put her hands on her hips as she looked back in the direction of Sunflower Grove. "I don't need them. I don't need anyone. I'd rather be alone than have friends who get mad at me and ignore me. I'm not going back."

"Won't you miss them?" Hal tipped his head to the side.

"Not even a little bit." She smiled as she looked at Hal. "I'm done with being cheerful too. I'm going to hide out in the woods so that no one can ever be mean to me again."

"It's worked for me so far." Hal shrugged. "But..." He sighed.

"What? What is it?" She frowned. "Are you angry at me now?"

"No, I'm not angry. I just think—well, maybe it's not so great being all alone." His wide eyes widened even more. "I didn't know how nice it would be to have a friend. Now that I do, I'm glad I met you, Ginger. Maybe friends are more important than what I thought."

"Good friends." She smiled. "Like you, Hal. Not like my friends in Sunflower Grove. Like you said, they weren't really friends at all."

"You know, if it weren't for you, I never would have left my home. I never would have touched the water in the waterfall." He huffed.

"I know, I'm sorry. It was a bad idea. You shouldn't have listened to me." She shook her head.

"No, it was a wonderful idea. I've never felt more alive. Yes, it was risky. Yes, I did get hurt. But it was worth it. Now I know what that water feels like on my feathers and I can't wait to try it again. But next time I'll be more careful." He flew up into the air. "Maybe being cheerful isn't so bad, Ginger. You sure cheered me up!"

"I did?" She laughed as she watched him zig and zag between the trees.

"You did." He zoomed down to the ground and landed in front of her.

"I do like to look on the brighter side of things." She smiled. "It just makes me feel good to think that things will work out, that everything will be just fine or even great!"

"There's nothing wrong with feeling good. Who would want to feel bad?" Hal flew up into the air. "I'll race you to the waterfall!"

"I'm going to win this time! I know it!" Ginger laughed as she flew after him. She flapped her wings as hard and fast as she could. Hal still flew much faster.

"I'll never beat him!" Ginger sighed. Then she flapped her wings faster. "But I'm still going to try!"

Hal reached a tangle of thick branches that he couldn't fly past. He had to go under them, while Ginger flew right through the tiny holes. This let her get to the waterfall before Hal.

"I won!" She cheered as Hal swooped in behind her.

"Good job." Hal laughed. "Now I'm going to try this wing-dipping thing again, but this time, I'll skip the rocky landing."

"Good idea." Ginger dipped her toes in the water.

She and Hal spent most of the day splashing and playing in the waterfall. As the sun began to set, she nestled in his feathers and looked up at the sky. "It really is beautiful isn't it?"

"Friendship? Yes." Hal smiled.

"I meant the sky." She laughed.

"Oh yes, that's beautiful too. I've never stayed awake all day before. It was fun!" He stretched his wings. "But now don't you think it's time to get back to your friends, Ginger?"

"My friends? What do you mean?" She flew up off his stomach and into the air. "They aren't my friends."

"Maybe they are. When you first landed on my branch, I

told you I would never be your friend. But now I am." He shrugged. "Maybe friendship is more important than one bad day."

"But I went back and no one wanted to see me! No, Hal, I'm staying here now—with you." She spread her arms for a hug. "Oh, wait, I promised I wouldn't." She frowned.

"Alright, maybe just this once." Hal wiggled his wings.

Ginger hugged him tight. She was glad that she had a new friend. But she really did miss her friends in Sunflower Grove.

CHAPTER 10

Ginger fell asleep on the branch outside of Hal's home. He offered for her to come inside, but it was a tight fit and she wanted to be under the stars. Not long after she fell asleep, she woke up to two big eyes staring down at her.

"Ginger!"

"Cara?" She blinked as she sat up.

"We have been looking everywhere for you!" Cara huffed as she looked at Ginger. "How could you just disappear like that? Do you know how worried we've all been?"

"I didn't think anyone would care." Ginger frowned.

"How could you ever think that?" Cara landed in front of Ginger. "We thought something terrible had happened to you. You had us all so scared!" She stomped one foot on the ground. "We were out all night and all day looking for you. Why would you do something like that to us?"

Ginger crept back along the branch. So that was why no one had helped her the night before. No one was there to help her. They had all been out looking for her. It seemed she had only made things worse.

Cara hardly ever lost her temper. She was just as angry as

Bella had been before Ginger had left. Surely, they wouldn't want her back now.

"I'm sorry, Cara." She sniffled. "Bella was so angry at me for being too cheerful. I just thought everyone would be happier if I was gone."

"That's ridiculous!" Cara stomped her foot against the branch. "Bella never should have talked to you like that, but you know how it is when fairies don't fly. They get cranky." She flew up into the air and waved her hand. "Ava! Ava, I found her! She's over here!"

Ginger cringed at the thought of how angry Ava might be.

As her heart began to sink, she remembered how angry Hal was with her when she'd first landed on his tree. He didn't want to have anything to do with her. But when he calmed down, he'd turned into a wonderful friend. She couldn't just assume that Cara would always be angry at her. She was still the same friend that Ginger had loved for so long.

"Cara, please, I know that you're angry with me, but I didn't mean to cause anyone any trouble. I was upset and I thought I would feel better if I was all alone." She sighed. "I didn't realize my cheerfulness bothered everyone."

"Oh, Ginger, I'm not mad at you. I mean, I am—maybe a little." Cara frowned. "But that's only because I was so scared. I didn't realize that Bella upset you so much. You usually don't get upset about anything."

"I try not to." Ginger shrugged. "I always want to look at the brighter side of things, but Bella was so mean. She hurt my feelings and then it was like I couldn't see the bright side of anything anymore."

"There you are, Ginger." Ava landed on the branch beside Cara. "She's here!" She shot a rocket of fairy dust off into the air. Soon all the fairies from Sunflower Grove gathered on the branch around Ginger.

"I'm so sorry, everyone." Ginger wiped at her eyes. "I didn't mean to make you worry. I just didn't think that you wanted me around."

"Why would you feel that way?" Ava looked into Ginger's eyes.

"It's my fault." Bella stepped forward and hung her head. "I said some very mean things to Ginger. I'm sorry, Ginger." She looked up at her friend. "I didn't mean anything I said. I was just really cranky."

"Really?" Ginger looked at her. "You didn't mean it?"

"No. I was just so frustrated at being cooped up. I'm sorry I wasn't a very good friend to you. Please come home, Ginger. It wouldn't be the same without you." Bella flung her arms around her.

Ginger's heart filled with joy. Her friends did want her back.

"I promise, I'll try not to be so cheerful."

"Please, don't promise that." Ava shook her head. "Ginger, you always have something bright and cheerful to say. That's a special gift that you give all of us. Even when things are very hard, you find a way to brighten all our moods."

"But I didn't brighten Bella's mood." Ginger shook her head. "I don't want to upset anyone."

"Sometimes people do get upset, Ginger. Sometimes, even the best of friends can say or do something that hurts our feelings. We can all get a little cranky. But that doesn't mean there's anything wrong with you." Ava touched Ginger's cheek lightly. "Your good attitude keeps Sunflower Grove bright and warm, and we wouldn't want you to be any other way."

"You mean it?" Ginger's eyes widened. "Are you sure?"

"I'm sure." Ava glanced at the other fairies. "What about the rest of you?"

"Absolutely!" Missy called out.

"We love you just the way you are, Ginger!" Fifi flew up into the air, wobbled, then landed in a pile on the branch. "Oof."

"Don't worry, Fifi, you'll get that landing one of these days, and when you do, you'll be so happy!" Ginger flew over to give her a hug.

"Thanks, Ginger." Fifi grinned as her friend helped her to her feet.

"Winged beasts!" A shriek came from inside the hole in the tree.

"Who's that?" Missy gulped and flew up into the air.

"It's okay, it's my friend Hal." Ginger smiled.

"There are so many of you!" Hal stuck his head out of the hole and peered at them. Then he gasped at the sight of sparkles on the leaves and branches of the tree. "And there is fairy dust everywhere!"

"Don't be angry, Hal!" Ginger pleaded. "We'll clean it up, I promise!"

"I'm not angry." Hal smiled as he ruffled his feathers. "I think it's wonderful."

"You do?" Ginger laughed. "I thought you weren't very fond of fairies?"

"That was until I had the chance to meet one. Now, any friend of my fairy friend Ginger, is a friend of mine too." He waved his wing at all the fairies gathered together. "I hope that we can all be friends."

"We certainly can." Missy smiled as she flew over to him. "You have beautiful feathers."

"Why, thank you." He fluffed them. "I'm quite proud of them."

"Ginger, you make friends everywhere you go." Bella laughed. She held her hand out to her friend. "Will you forgive me for being so mean?"

"Of course I will. I mean, after all, if you hadn't said those things, I never would have met Hal." Ginger smiled at him. "I guess there really is a bright side to everything."

"Thanks to you, there is." Ava gave Ginger a warm hug. "Please remember, even if it seems as if one of us is angry with you, that doesn't mean that we don't love you. Even when your feelings are hurt, it's important to look for the bright side."

"From now on I always will." Ginger hugged Ava back and smiled.

Not only did she have her fairy friends back, she had a wonderful new friend as well. Things would be just fine—or even great—from now on!

AVAILABLE IN AUDIO

PJ Ryan books for kids are also available as audiobooks.

Visit the author website for a complete list at: PJRyanBooks.com

You can also listen to free audio samples there.

Made in United States
North Haven, CT
21 March 2022

17392060R00143